Friedrich Dürrenmatt

THE INSPECTOR BARLACH MYSTERIES

THE JUDGE AND HIS HANGMAN

AND

SUSPICION

TRANSLATED BY JOEL AGEE

WITH A FOREWORD BY SVEN BIRKERTS

THE UNIVERSITY OF CHICAGO PRESS

CHICAGO · LONDON

Publication of this work was made possible through the generous support of Pro Helvetia, the Arts Council of Switzerland

www.prohelvetia.ch

The University of Chicago Press, Chicago 60637
The University of Chicago Press, Ltd., London
Foreword © 2006 by Sven Birkerts
English-language translation by Joel Agee © 2006 by Diogenes Verlag AG, Zürich
© 1986 by Diogenes Verlag AG, Zürich
Printed in the United States of America

17 16 15 14 13   5   6
ISBN-13: 978-0-226-17444-0 (paper)
ISBN-10: 0-226-17444-1 (paper)

The Judge and His Hangman was originally published as *Der Richter und sein Henker* (1950) in *Der Schweizerische Beobachter* (1950/51), and revised by Benziger Verlag, Einsiedeln, Zurich (1952).

Suspicion was originally published as *Der Verdacht* (1951) in *Der Schweizerische Beobachter* (1951/52), and revised by Benziger Verlag, Einsiedeln, Zurich (1953).

Library of Congress Cataloging-in-Publication Data

Dürrenmatt, Friedrich.
    [Richter und sein Henker. English]
    The Inspector Barlach mysteries : The judge and his hangman and Suspicion / Friedrich Dürrenmatt ; translated by Joel Agee ; with a foreword by Sven Birkerts.
        p.   cm.
    ISBN-13: 978-0-226-17444-0 (pbk. : alk. paper)
    ISBN-10: 0-226-17444-1 (pbk. : alk. paper)
    I. Dürrenmatt, Friedrich. Verdacht. English. II. Agee, Joel. III. Birkerts, Sven. IV. Title.
    V. Title: Judge and his hangman. VI. Title: Suspicion.

PT2607.U493R513 2006
833'.914—dc22

                                                        2006021610

♾ The paper used in this publication meets the minimum requirements of the American National Standard for Information Sciences—Permanence of Paper for Printed Library Materials, ANSI Z39.48-1992.

CONTENTS

FOREWORD

Friedrich Dürrenmatt (1921–1990) is probably most widely known as the author of inventive and edgily paradoxical plays like *The Visit* and *The Physicists,* but in fact these were only part of his enterprise. The full resume also boasts novels, essays and polemics, and several utterly sui generis detective novels. These latter, represented here by *The Judge and the Hangman* and *Suspicion,* both featuring the ailing and curmudgeonly Inspector Barlach, find surprising ways to subvert the expectations of their genre. They are packaged as entertainments, but theirs is less a lightness of purpose than of execution: they play through complex moral issues with a speed-chess decisiveness and inexorability. This lightness, I think, is European; part of the tradition of idea-testing that Milan Kundera has insisted is one of the main prerogatives of the novel. Working here with the reduced encumbrances of the genre—little characterization or psychologizing—Dürrenmatt can exercise his dramatic instinct on the most vexing ethical questions.

Dürrenmatt is a philosopher-moralist by temperament, intent on exploring what he sees as a perpetual confrontation of good and evil. If the police procedural seems an unlikely form, we should recall what Dostoevsky accomplished with *Crime and Punishment.* That Dürrenmatt is Swiss, not Russian, does not bar him from expressing his own brand of intensity. Having come of age in the long

Walpurgisnacht of World War II, and then nourished on the bitter milk of postwar existentialism, he is in these early works obsessed with what the textbooks have tagged the European "crisis in values."

Like any writer preoccupied with good versus evil, moral order versus nihilism, Dürrenmatt tends toward binary ways of thinking, but never in reductionist ways—he makes consistently clever use of doubles, reversals, and the dynamic possibilities of paradox. These two novels, *The Judge and the Hangman* (1950) and *Suspicion* (1951), show him moving his way across the spectrum of inquiry, from the realist grounding of the former, to the more expressionistic boundary-pushing of the latter. Both novellas bring the contest of values to a high pitch, and while each ultimately gives the nod to the white hats, in neither case is it by more than a hair's breadth. This accounts for a good part of the dramatic tension of the works—we are never quite assured of the certainty of the deeper outcome.

Inspector Barlach, though a slightly caricatured "type," exerts greater presence and force than we might expect from a collection of attributes. *The Judge and the Hangman,* the earlier of the novellas, introduces a detective at career's end, a man with a failing body who has been told that even with a necessary surgery he has but a year to live. Barlach is set starkly before us—no family, a domestic life no more furnished than Sam Spade's, with only gruff and grumbling ties to his colleagues on the Bern police force. This, together with his death's-door alienation from the business of living, injects all developments with ominous gravity.

The crime: a police officer is found shot in his car on a Swiss country road. Killer and motive are unknown, but the trail of the investigation, which I won't try to summarize here, leads the Inspector and his associate toward a shadowy power-broker named Gastmann. Dürrenmatt choreographs an ever-surprising play of revelation and reversal—the expected delights of the genre—but he also makes it clear that Barlach is not much concerned with the usual business of tracking clues. He has another interest: for him it is the case behind the case, the investigation as the playing out of an ancient wager.

As it turns out, Barlach and the suspect were once great comrades. They continue to share a deep mutual understanding, but their once-fond feeling has warped into the cold sarcastic decorum of archrivals. When they meet in the course of the investigation and relive their early connection, much comes clear. There was a night in a tavern in the Bosphorus: the friends were young, drinking, challenging each other with their philosophies. Gastmann returns to the scene in memory. "What did we talk about, Barlach, in the rot of that bar in a suburb called Tophane, swathed in Turkish cigarette smoke?" He begins to lecture his adversary. "Your thesis was that human imperfection—the fact that we can never predict with certainty how others will act, and that furthermore we have no way of calculating how chance interferes in our plans—guarantees that most crimes will perforce be detected. To commit a crime, you said, is an act of stupidity, because you can't operate with people as if they were chessmen. Against this I contended . . . that it's precisely this incalculable, chaotic element in human relations that makes it possible to commit crimes that *cannot* be detected, and that for this reason the majority of crimes are not only not punished, but are simply not known, because, in effect, they are perfectly hidden."

From this follows a wager: Barlach's friend vows to commit a crime in Barlach's presence without his being able to prove he did it. The mutual challenge seems to liberate the dormant nature of each; the would-be criminal coming to embrace a full-blown nihilism, the signature of which, as in *Crime and Punishment,* is the gratuitous act—a murder enacted without compunction or pressing reason—and his opponent, Barlach, upholding the social contract, its assumption of an essential morality.

Chess again—only the Inspector has been embroiled in this particular game over a long lifetime. Dürrenmatt has staged it so that the end of the novel brings us to the end of the game, but while rulebook chess has the stalemate option, the moral philosopher demands a resolution.

The final outcome is a victory, but for Barlach it brings little sense of reward, only a staying of what would have to be a larger calamity. Moreover, when the case is concluded, he has to confront his situation once again: "The enormous avid vitality that had flared up in him was collapsing and threatened to die altogether." At novel's end it is clear that the Inspector's last chance is to take the surgery—a short-term gamble. Either way, the outlook is grim. Why then do we finish with a sense of uplift? I think it is that Barlach has reaffirmed, if barely, the idea of the durability of decency.

With *Suspicion*, Dürrenmatt changes the mode of his presentation. He more or less eliminates all but one basic set—the hospital bed—and at the same time he raises the stakes. If the earlier novella examined the conflict between moral value and nihilism from a more individual perspective, here the author searches for implications on a historical/cultural level. To do so he bends the bars of his narration outward, situating events on what feels like the fringe of plausibility—a bold step to take, given the relatively stable constraints of the detective genre.

As in *The Judge and the Hangman*, Dürrenmatt plays his scenes out quickly, creating momentum while keeping himself free of the burdens of explication: the buzzer sounds and the game is on. As the novella opens, Barlach is in the Salem, a hospital in Bern, recuperating from the procedure that was to have prolonged his life. The man is exhausted, diminished. But he is not completely without the vital sign of his investigative curiosity; the merest prompt is enough to engage the old reflexes.

What happens is this: Barlach is showing his physician, Dr. Hungertobel, a photograph in a *Life* magazine he has been perusing. It was taken at the Stutthof concentration camp and a certain Dr. Nehle is pictured operating on a prisoner without anesthesia. Hungertobel turns pale when he sees the photograph, but says nothing to Barlach. He leaves the room in an agitated state. When Barlach later presses him on the matter, the beginnings of a story—and mystery—emerge. Hungertobel explains that he thought he had recognized the face of an old friend, a Doctor Emmenberger, but then realized he had made a mistake: his friend had been living in Chile when the photograph was taken. Still . . .

Naturally, a question about exchanged identities comes up, the upshot being that given the resemblance it is just possible that the legendarily sadistic camp doctor may be alive and well, posing as Dr. Emmenberger and "treating" wealthy patients in an exclusive facility outside the city. Barlach, bedridden, now mere days from his retirement, is moved to make a curious request of a fellow policeman. He asks him to go to the bookshop of one Feitelbach and request a copy of *Gulliver's Travels.* "The book with the dwarves and the giants?" his associate inquires. "Barlach laughed: 'You see, Blatter, I just love fairy tales.'"

This is one fairy tale that not even the dark-minded Brothers Grimm could have conjured to the page. First there comes a visit, at night, by way of the hospital window, of a giant named, yes, Gulliver—the book order was a special summons through a friend. Gulliver, a Jew, a camp survivor, is a surreally anomalous figure. Near monstrous in size, utterly driven in demeanor (he guzzles vodka all day long), Gulliver knew Nehle—the doctor had operated on him, as on so many others, without use of anesthetic. But the giant believes that the man took his life in Hamburg several years ago, when the photo was printed. Indeed, it had been Gulliver who passed the photo to the press.

Nehle, he explains to Barlach, was a peculiar kind of torturer. "Nehle only operated on Jews who volunteered," Gulliver says, "who knew exactly what awaited them, who even, this was his condition, had to watch operations to see the full horror of the torture before they could give their consent to suffer through the same thing." Barlach demands to know why. "Hope," answers the giant. People consented because they believed they would be freed afterward. The Inspector is confused. "What sort of a man was Nehle?" Gulliver can't answer his question, saying only: "How often I tried to fathom what went on behind his glittering spectacles." But the import seems clear enough. Trading in hope, Nehle is finally the most heartless of sadists—he vivisects the spirit as well as the body.

Barlach arranges to have himself checked in to Emmenberger's clinic—a predictably sterile, chillingly efficient place. He is hoping to be incognito, of course, but his pretense collapses immediately. The man with the glittering spectacles knows exactly who he is and why he has come: straightaway the Inspector is sequestered and drugged, rendered essentially captive. He finds himself entering a fearful dreamworld where the days and nights pass in a haze while he awaits his medical examination. He has to battle to keep his focus. And he succeeds—enough. Observing Emmenberger and his drug-addicted nurse/mistress, Barlach arrives at the truth about the doctor's identity and his perverse game. But at the same time Barlach grows weaker, more vulnerable. It looks very unlikely that he will get out of the clinic alive.

I won't spoil the prospective reader's anxious pleasure by detailing the twists and intensifications Dürrenmatt uses to bring *Suspicion* to its resolution. Nor will I disclose his surprise interventions, except to say that it is with these that he comes very close to abandoning the realist conventions of the genre. But the matter is more complex—and interesting—than any mere deployment of a deus ex machina device to reverse a seemingly foregone outcome. If that were all, the novel would be nothing but a literary sleight of hand.

What gives the author permission—and what is in a larger sense the point of the novella—is the fact that with the Nazi camps, their scale and their mind-stopping sadism, history itself departed all human bounds, even beyond the extreme allowances we make for the cruelties of war. Human nature surpassed its former limits—collectively—revealing once and for all our potential for depravity. In a sense, all value, all idea of an anchored human foundation, has henceforth been followed by a question mark. Nehle, we understand, is but one instance, and his struggle with Barlach is a test case, a way for Dürrenmatt to play out the endgame scenario. That Barlach should be brought to the very brink of death is a measure of the potency of evil; that he should not rescue himself but *be* rescued in the way he is can be construed as a deeply ambiguous resolution.

But if Dürrenmatt is essentially pessimistic in his assessment of the primary standoff, and its long-term outlook, his way of staging the situation is significant. By working the issue through as he does, as a kind of genre puzzle, he claims the moral agon as a subject for a more popular art. Is this an exploitation of what should only be addressed in more demanding works—works like Thomas Mann's *Dr. Faustus*, say? In an argument my first impulse might be to say that it is. Tragedy does not assimilate easily to genre constraints. But after reading these novellas I make an exception: Dürrenmatt's essential seriousness of purpose survives the swiftness and narrative lightness of his approach. Successfully anchoring the drama in the sphere of values, he goads us to widen the genre frame by degrees— widen until it fits the big picture.

THE JUDGE AND HIS HANGMAN

I

On the morning of November third, 1948, Alphons Clenin, the policeman of the village of Twann, came upon a blue Mercedes parked by the side of the highway right by the woods where the road from Lamboing comes out of the Twann River gorge. It was one of those foggy mornings of which there were many in that late fall, and Clenin had already walked past the car when he decided to have another look. He had casually glanced through the clouded windows and had the impression that he had seen the driver slumped over the wheel. Being a decent and levelheaded fellow, he immediately assumed the man was drunk and decided to give him a helping hand instead of a summons. He would wake him, drive him to Twann, and sober him up with some soup and black coffee at the Bear Inn. For while drunk driving was forbidden by law, drunk sleeping in a stationary car by the side of the road was not forbidden. Clenin opened the door and laid a fatherly hand on the stranger's shoulder. At that moment he noticed that the man was dead. He had been shot through the temples. And now Clenin saw that the door by the passenger seat was unlatched. There was little blood in the car and the dead man's dark-gray coat wasn't even stained. The gleaming edge of a yellow wallet stuck out of the inside pocket. Clenin pulled it out and had no trouble establishing that the dead man was Ulrich Schmied, a police lieutenant from Bern.

Clenin didn't quite know what to do. As a village policeman, he had never had to deal with violence of this magnitude. He paced back and forth by the side of the road. When the rising sun broke through the mist and shone on the corpse, it made him uncomfortable. He went back to the car, picked up the gray felt hat that lay at the dead man's feet, and pulled it down over his head until he could no longer see the pierced temples. Now he felt better.

The policeman again crossed over to the side of the road facing Twann, and wiped the sweat from his forehead. Then he made a decision. He shifted the dead man onto the passenger seat, carefully propped him up, fastened him with a leather strap he found in the back of the car, and sat down behind the wheel.

The motor wouldn't start, but Clenin easily coasted the car down the steep road to Twann and stopped by the gas station in front of the Bear. The attendant never noticed that the distinguished-looking man sitting motionless in the front seat was dead. That was just fine with Clenin. He hated scandals.

But as he drove along the edge of the lake toward Biel, the fog thickened again, the sun disappeared, and the morning turned dark as Judgment Day. Clenin found himself in a long line of cars that for some inexplicable reason were driving even more slowly than the weather required. Almost like a funeral procession, he thought involuntarily. The corpse sat motionless at his side, except for moments when a bump in the road made him nod like an Oriental sage. This made Clenin less and less inclined to pass the cars ahead of him. They reached Biel much later than he had expected.

While the routine investigation of the Schmied case got under way in Biel, the sad facts were conveyed to Inspector Barlach, who had been the dead man's superior in Bern.

Barlach had lived abroad for many years and had made a name for himself as a criminologist, first in Constantinople and later in Germany. His last job there had been as chief of the crime division of the Frankfurt am Main police, but he had come back to his native city as early as 1933. The reason for his return was not his love of Bern—his golden grave, as he often called it—but a slap he had given a high-ranking official of the new German government. This vicious assault was the talk of Frankfurt for a while. Opinions in Bern, always sensitive to the shifts in European politics, judged it first as an inexcusable outrage, then as a deplorable but understandable act, and finally—in 1945—as the only possible thing a Swiss could have done.

Barlach's first action in the Schmied case was to instruct his subordinates to maintain complete secrecy for the first few days—an order which it took all his prestige and authority to enforce. "We know too little," he said, "and besides, newspapers are the most superfluous invention of the last two thousand years."

Barlach evidently expected this secret procedure to bring results, in contrast to his "boss," Dr. Lucius Lutz, who lectured in criminology at the university. This official, the son of an ancient Bern family who owed their fortune to the beneficent interference of a rich uncle from Basel, had just returned from a visit to the police departments of New York and Chicago and was "appalled at the antediluvian state of crime prevention in the federal capital of Switzerland," as he publicly stated to Police Commissioner Freiberger on the occasion of a joint ride home in the streetcar.

That same morning, after another call to the Biel police, Barlach paid a visit to the Schönlers, the family in whose house on Bantigerstrasse Schmied had rented a room. As usual, he walked through the old part of town and across the Nydegg bridge, for in his opinion Bern was much too small a city for "streetcars and suchlike."

Climbing the stone steps at Haspelstrasse tired him a little. Moments like this had a way of reminding him that he was over sixty. But soon he found himself at his destination and rang the bell.

It was Frau Schönler herself who opened the door, a short, fat lady not without a certain distinction and dignity. She immediately let Barlach in, for she knew him.

"Schmied had to go away on business last night," Barlach said. "He had to leave quickly, so he asked me to send something on to him. Kindly take me to his room, Frau Schönler."

The lady nodded, and they walked down the hall past a picture in a heavy gold frame. Barlach glanced at it; it was Böcklin's *Island of the Dead.*

"So where is Herr Schmied?" the fat woman asked as she opened the room.

"Abroad," Barlach said, looking up at the ceiling.

The room was on the ground floor, with a view through a doorway onto a small garden planted with old brown fir trees that were apparently sick, for the ground was densely covered with needles. No doubt this was the best room in the house. Barlach went to the desk and looked around once more. One of the dead man's ties lay on the couch.

"He's gone to the tropics, hasn't he, Herr Barlach," Frau Schönler asked, unable to suppress her curiosity. The question startled him. "No, he's not in the tropics, he's a bit higher up."

Frau Schönler opened her eyes wide and clapped her hands over her head. "My God! In the Himalayas?"

"Close," Barlach said. "You almost guessed it." He opened a folder that was lying on the desk and immediately tucked it under his arm.

"Did you find what you wanted to send Herr Schmied?"

"I did."

He looked around again, avoiding a second glance at the necktie.

"He is the best tenant we have ever had, and there has never been any trouble with lady visitors and such," Frau Schönler assured him.

Barlach went to the door. "I'll send an officer around now and then or come by myself. Schmied has some other important documents that we may need."

"Do you think he'll send me a postcard from abroad?" Frau Schönler wanted to know. "My son collects stamps."

Barlach looked at Frau Schönler with a pensive frown. "It's very unlikely," he said. "Policemen usually don't send postcards when they're traveling on duty. It's not allowed."

Thereupon Frau Schönler again clapped her hands over her head and remarked with exasperation, "The things they forbid nowadays!"

Barlach left and was glad to leave the house behind him.

2

Deeply absorbed in thought, he ate his lunch in the Café du Théâtre instead of his favorite restaurant, the Schmiedstube, leafing through Schmied's folder as he ate and reading some pages with close attention. Then, after a brief walk along the Bundesterrasse, he returned to his office at two o'clock, where he was informed that Schmied's body had arrived from Biel. However, he decided not to pay a visit to his former subordinate. He did not much care for corpses and therefore generally left them in peace. He would have also gladly done without a visit to Lutz, but this one he could not avoid. He carefully locked Schmied's folder in his desk without examining it any further, lit a cigar, and went to Lutz's office, well knowing how Lutz always resented the liberty the old man took by smoking in his room. Only once, years ago, had Lutz dared to object, but Barlach with a dismissive gesture replied that he had served ten years in Turkey and had always smoked in the offices of his superiors in Constantinople, a remark that carried all the more weight in that there was no way to disprove it.

Dr. Lucius Lutz received Barlach nervously, since in his opinion nothing had yet been done, and offered him a comfortable chair near his desk.

"No news from Biel yet?" Barlach asked.

"Nothing yet," Lutz replied.

"I wonder why not," Barlach said. "They're working like crazy."

Barlach sat down and glanced at the pictures by Traffelet on the walls, tinted pen-and-ink drawings of soldiers under a large waving flag, sometimes with a general, sometimes without, marching either from left to right or else from right to left.

"It is an alarming," Lutz began, "indeed an increasingly frightening thing to behold the degree to which criminology in this country is still in its infancy. God knows I'm used to inefficiency in our canton, but the procedure that is evidently considered the natural course to take in the case of a murdered police lieutenant casts such an appalling light on the professional competence of our village police that I am still horrified."

"Rest assured, Dr. Lutz," Barlach replied, "our village police are as fit for their job as the police in Chicago, and I'm certain we'll find out who killed Schmied."

"Do you have someone in mind as a suspect, Inspector Barlach?"

Barlach gazed at Lutz for a long time and finally said, "Yes, I have someone in mind, Doctor Lutz."

"Whom?"

"I can't tell you yet."

"Well, that's very interesting," Lutz said, "I know that you are always prepared, Inspector Barlach, to prettify some blunder committed in disregard of modern scientific criminology. But don't forget that time marches on and will not stop for anyone, not even for the most famous criminologist. I have seen crimes in New York and Chicago the likes of which you in our dear old Bern have never imagined. But now a police lieutenant has been murdered, and that is a sure sign that here too, the walls of public security are beginning to crack, and surely that calls for ruthless measures."

"Certainly," Barlach replied, "that is what I am doing."

"Well, I'm glad to hear that," Lutz replied.

A clock was ticking on the wall.

Barlach gingerly pressed his left hand on his belly and with his right hand extinguished his cigar in the ashtray Lutz had set before him. He told Lutz that for some time now he had not been in the best of health, and that his doctor was starting to worry about him.

It was stomach trouble, he said, and he would be grateful if Dr. Lutz would appoint someone who could assist him with the legwork in the Schmied murder case, so that Barlach could work from his desk. Lutz agreed. "Whom do you want as your assistant?"

"Tschanz," Barlach said. "He's on vacation in the Bernese Oberland, but we could recall him."

Lutz replied, "Good idea. Tschanz is a man who works hard at keeping up with the latest advances in criminology."

Then he turned his back on Barlach and gazed out the window at the broad expanse of the Waisenhausplatz, which was full of children.

Suddenly he felt an irresistible urge to argue with Barlach about the value of modern scientific criminology. He turned around, but Barlach had already left.

Even though it was close to five already, Barlach decided to drive to the scene of the crime. He took Blatter along, a tall bloated policeman who never spoke a word, whom Barlach liked for that reason, and who also drove the car. In Twann they were welcomed by Clenin, who was looking defiant in anticipation of a reprimand. But the inspector was friendly, shook his hand and said it was a pleasure to meet a man who knew how to think for himself. These words made Clenin proud, though he wasn't quite sure what the old man meant by them. He led Barlach up the road toward the scene of the crime. Blatter lagged behind, disgruntled at having to walk.

Barlach wondered about the name of the town, Lamboing.

"It's Lamlingen in German," Clenin informed him.

"I see," said Barlach. "That sounds much better."

They arrived at the scene of the murder. On their right, the side of the road facing Twann was lined by a wall.

"Where was the car, Clenin?"

"Here," the policeman replied, pointing at the pavement, "almost in the middle of the road," and, since Barlach was hardly paying any attention, "Maybe it would have been better if I had left the car here with the body inside."

"Why?" Barlach asked, looking up at the cliffs of the Jura mountains. "The dead should be removed as quickly as possible, there's no reason why they should stick around. You were right to drive Schmied back to Biel."

Barlach stepped to the edge of the road and looked down over Twann. There was nothing but vineyards between him and the old village. The sun had already set. The road curved like a snake between the houses, and a long freight train stood waiting in the station.

"Didn't anyone hear anything down there, Clenin?" he asked. "The village is nearby. You would hear a shot."

"No one heard anything except the sound of the motor running all night, and no one thought that meant anything bad had happened."

"Of course not, why would they." He looked at the vineyards again. "How is the wine this year, Clenin?"

"Good. We could try some."

"Yes, I would very much like a glass of new wine."

And he struck against something hard with his right foot. He bent down and picked up a small, longish piece of metal flattened in the front, and held it between his thin fingers. Clenin and Blatter leaned in to look at it more closely.

"A bullet," Blatter said. "From a pistol."

"You've done it again, Inspector!" Clenin said admiringly.

"Just a coincidence," Barlach said, and they walked down the road toward Twann.

3

Apparently the new wine did not agree with Barlach, for he declared the next morning that he had been throwing up all night. Lutz, who met the inspector on the stairs, was genuinely concerned for his well-being and advised him to go the doctor.

"Sure, sure," Barlach mumbled, adding that he liked doctors even less than modern scientific criminology.

Once he was in his office he felt better. He sat down behind his desk, unlocked his drawer, and pulled out the dead man's folder.

At ten o'clock—Barlach was still immersed in his reading—Tschanz came to see him. He had returned from his vacation late the previous night.

Barlach started at the sight of him. For a moment it had seemed as if the dead Schmied had come into the room. Tschanz was wearing the same coat as Schmied's and a similar felt hat. Only the round and good-natured face was different.

"Good thing you're here, Tschanz," Barlach said. "We have to discuss the Schmied case. You'll have to take over most of the job, I'm not well."

"Yes, I've already heard," said Tschanz.

Tschanz pulled up a chair and sat down, resting his left arm on Barlach's desk. Schmied's folder was lying open on the desk.

Barlach leaned back in his chair. "To you I can speak frankly," he began. "I've come across thousands of policemen, good ones and bad ones, between Constantinople and Bern. Many were no better than the poor bastards we populate the jails with, except that they happen to be on the other side of the law. But Schmied was in a class of his own, he had real talent. He could have put us all in his pocket. He had a clear mind, he knew what he wanted, and he kept it to himself. He spoke only when it was necessary. We have to emulate him, Tschanz, he was way ahead of us."

Tschanz slowly turned his head toward Barlach, for he had been looking out the window, and said, "That could be."

Barlach saw that he was not convinced.

"We don't know much about his death," the inspector continued, "this bullet is all we've got." And he told him where he had found the bullet, and placed it on the desk. Tschanz picked it up and looked at it.

"It's from an army pistol," he said, and returned the bullet.

Barlach closed the folder on his desk. "Above all, we don't know what Schmied was doing in Twann or Lamlingen. He never had an assignment to the Lake Biel area, I would have known about that. We don't have even a remotely probable motive for his driving out there."

Tschanz, who was only half listening to what Barlach was saying, crossed his legs and said, "All we know is how Schmied was murdered."

"And how would you know that?" the inspector asked, not without surprise, after a pause.

"The steering wheel on Schmied's car is on the left, and you found the bullet on the left side of the road, as seen from the car; and the people in Twann heard the motor running all night. Schmied was stopped by the killer as he was driving from Lamboing to Twann. He probably knew the killer, otherwise he wouldn't have stopped. Schmied opened the door on the right to let the killer in and sat back behind the wheel. At that moment he was shot. Schmied must have been unaware that the man intended to kill him."

Barlach considered this interpretation. Then he said, "Now I'll have a cigar after all," and then, after lighting it, "You are right, Tschanz, that's more or less what must have happened, I'm willing to believe that. But this still doesn't explain what Schmied was doing on the road between Twann and Lamlingen."

Tschanz pointed out that Schmied had been wearing evening clothes under his overcoat.

"He did? I didn't know that," Barlach said.

"But haven't you seen the body?"

"No, I don't like corpses."

"But it was in the official record."

"I like official records even less."

Tschanz said nothing.

But Barlach remarked, "This just makes the case more complicated. What was Schmied doing wearing a tuxedo by the Twann River gorge?"

"On the contrary," Tschanz replied, "it could simplify the case. I'm sure there aren't many people around Lamboing who are rich enough to give black tie parties."

He drew out a small pocket calendar and explained that it had belonged to Schmied.

"I've seen it," Barlach nodded. "There's nothing in it of any importance."

Tschanz contradicted him. "For Wednesday, November second, Schmied had entered a G. It was on that day that he was killed, shortly before midnight, according to the coroner. Then there's another G on Wednesday the twenty-sixth, and again on Tuesday, October eighteenth."

"G could mean all sorts of things," Barlach said. "A woman's name, or anything."

"Hardly a woman's name," Tschanz replied. "Schmied's fiancée's name is Anna, and Schmied was a steady sort of guy."

"I don't know about her either," the inspector admitted; and seeing that Tschanz was surprised at his ignorance, he said, "All I'm interested in, Tschanz, is who killed Schmied."

"Of course," Tschanz replied politely. But then he shook his head and laughed, "You're a strange man, Inspector."

"I'm an old black tomcat who likes to eat mice." Barlach said this very seriously.

Tschanz didn't know what to say to that. Finally he replied, "On the days he marked with a G, Schmied put on his tuxedo and drove off in his Mercedes."

"Now how do you know that?"

"From Frau Schönler."

"I see," Barlach said and fell silent. But then he said, "Yes, these are facts."

Tschanz looked keenly into the commissioner's face, lit a cigarette, and said with some hesitation, "Dr. Lutz told me you have a definite suspicion."

"Yes, Tschanz, I do."

"Commissioner, since I have become your assistant in the Schmied murder case, don't you think it might be better if you told me who it is you're suspecting?"

"You see," Barlach answered slowly, deliberating each word as carefully as Tschanz did, "my suspicion is not a scientific criminological suspicion. I have no solid reasons to justify it. You have seen how little I know. All I have is an idea as to who the murderer might be; but the person I have in mind has yet to deliver the proof of his guilt."

"What do you mean, Inspector?" Tschanz asked.

Barlach smiled. "Simply that I have to wait for the evidence to emerge that will justify his arrest."

"If I am to work with you, I have to know who it is I'm targeting with my investigation," Tschanz declared politely.

"Above all we must remain objective. That applies to me, as the one who holds a suspicion, and to you, as the one who will conduct most of the inquest. I don't know whether my suspicion will be confirmed. I await the results of your investigation. It is your job to find Schmied's killer regardless of my suspicion. If the person I suspect is in fact the killer, you will find him in your own way—which, unlike mine, is impeccably scientific. And if I'm wrong, you will find the right man, and there will have been no need to know the name of the person I falsely suspected."

They were silent for a while, and then the old man asked, "Are you willing to work with me on this basis?"

Tschanz hesitated a moment before he replied, "All right, I agree."

"What do you want to do now, Tschanz?"

Tschanz walked over to the window. "There's a G on today's date in Schmied's calendar. I want to drive to Lamboing and see what I can find out. I'll leave at seven, the same time Schmied always left when he drove out there."

He turned around again and asked politely, but as if in jest, "Are you coming along, Inspector?"

"Yes, Tschanz, I'm coming along," was the unexpected reply.

"Very well," Tschanz said, a little bewildered, "seven o'clock."

In the doorway he turned around again. "You, too, paid Frau Schönler a visit, Inspector Barlach. Didn't you find anything there?"

The old man did not answer right away. First he locked the folder in the drawer of his desk and put the key in his pocket.

"No, Tschanz," he finally said, "I found nothing. You may go now."

4

At seven o'clock Tschanz drove to the riverside house in the Altenberg district where Inspector Barlach had lived since 1933. It was raining, and the speeding police car skidded in the curve by the Nydegg Bridge. But Tschanz quickly regained control. He drove slowly along the Altenbergstrasse, for he had never visited Barlach before, and he peered through the wet windows searching for the house number, which he deciphered with difficulty. He honked the horn several times; there was no sign of any movement inside. Tschanz left the car and hurried through the rain to the door. After a moment of hesitation he pressed down the door handle, since he couldn't see the bell in the dark. The door was open, and Tschanz stepped into a vestibule. He found himself facing a half-open door through which light fell into the hallway. He approached the door, knocked, and, receiving no answer, pushed it open. In front of him was a large room, its walls lined with books. Barlach was lying on a couch. The inspector was asleep, but he seemed prepared for the drive to Lake Biel, for he had his winter coat on. He was holding a book. The sound of Barlach's quiet breathing, the many books on their shelves, filled Tschanz with a deep unease. He looked around cautiously. The room had no windows, but each wall had a door that must lead to other rooms. In the middle of the floor stood a large desk, and on top of it—startling Tschanz the moment he saw it—lay a large brass snake.

"I brought that with me from Constantinople," said a quiet voice from the sofa, and Barlach sat up.

"You see, Tschanz, I already have my coat on. We can leave."

"Pardon me," Tschanz replied, still taken aback, "you were asleep and didn't hear me knocking. I couldn't find the bell."

"I don't have a bell. I don't need one; the door is never locked."

"Not even when you're out?"

"Not even when I'm out. It's always exciting to come home and see whether something's been stolen or not."

Tschanz laughed and picked up the snake from Constantinople.

"I was almost killed with that thing once," the inspector remarked somewhat sardonically, and only now did Tschanz notice that the snake's head could be used as a handle and that its body was as sharp as the blade of a knife. Baffled, he looked at the strange glittering ornaments on the terrible weapon. Barlach stood next to him.

"Be ye wise as serpents," he said, giving Tschanz a long and thoughtful look. Then he smiled, "And harmless as doves." And he tapped Tschanz lightly on the shoulder. "I've had some sleep, for the first time in days. Damned stomach."

"It's that bad?" Tschanz asked.

"It's that bad," the inspector coolly replied.

"You should stay home, Herr Barlach, it's cold outside and it's raining."

Barlach looked at Tschanz again and laughed, "Nonsense, there's a killer to be caught. It would suit you just fine if I stayed home, wouldn't it?"

As they were driving across the Nyddegg Bridge, Barlach asked, "Why don't you go by way of Aargauerstalden in the direction of Zollikofen, Tschanz? Isn't that quicker than going through the city?"

"Because I don't want to go to Twann via Zollikofen and Biel. I prefer to go via Kerzers and Erlach."

"That is an unusual route, Tschanz."

"It's not so unusual at all, Inspector."

They fell silent. The lights of the city glided past. But when they reached Bethlehem, Tschanz asked, "Did you ever drive with Schmied?"

"Yes, frequently. He was a careful driver." And Barlach cast a pensive glance at the speedometer, which showed almost a hundred and ten kilometers an hour.

Tschanz slowed down a little. "I remember driving with Schmied once, he was slow as hell, and he had a strange sort of name for his car. He used it when he had to stop for gas. Do you remember the name? I forgot it."

"He called his car the Blue Charon," Barlach replied.

"Charon is a name in Greek mythology, right?"

"Charon was the ferryman who took the dead to the underworld, Tschanz."

"Schmied had rich parents, so he got the kind of schooling people like us can't afford. That's why he knew about Charon and we don't."

Barlach put his hands in his coat pockets and looked at the speedometer again. "Yes, Tschanz," he said. "Schmied was well educated, he knew Greek and Latin, and with his college credits he had a great future, but nevertheless I wouldn't go over a hundred."

A little past Gummenen, the car pulled up sharply at a gas station. A man stepped out to attend them.

"Police," Tschanz said. "We need some information."

Indistinctly they saw a curious and somewhat alarmed face peering into the car.

"Do you remember a driver stopping here two days ago who called his car the blue Charon?"

The man shook his head in wonderment, and Tschanz drove on. "We'll ask the next one."

At the gas station in Kerzers, the attendant didn't know anything either.

Barlach grumbled, "This doesn't make any sense."

At Erlach Tschanz was lucky. On Wednesday evening someone like that had stopped for gas, he was told.

"You see," Tschanz said as they turned into the Neuenburg-Biel highway, "now we know that on Wednesday evening Schmied drove through Kerzers and Erlach."

"Are you sure?" asked the inspector.

"I just proved it you."

"Yes, it's perfectly proven. But what good will it do you, Tschanz?"

"It just is what it is. Every bit of knowledge helps."

"There you're right again," said the old man, looking out for Lake Biel. It was no longer raining. They had just passed Neuveville when the lake emerged among shreds of mist. They drove into Ligerz. Tschanz drove slowly, looking for the exit to Lamboing.

Now the car was climbing through the vineyards. Barlach opened the window and looked down at the lake. A few stars shone above Peters Island. The lights were reflected in the water, and a motorboat was racing across the lake. Late for this time of year, Barlach thought. Down in the valley before them lay Twann and behind them Ligerz.

They went around a curve and drove toward the woods, whose presence they sensed somewhere ahead of them in the night. Tschanz seemed a little unsure and wondered whether this might not be the road to Schernelz. When a man came walking toward them, he stopped. "Is this the way to Lamboing?"

"Just keep going and turn right by the white row of houses, straight into the forest." The man was wearing a leather jacket. He whistled to a small white dog with a black head that was skipping about in front of the headlights.

"Come along, Ping-Ping!"

They left the vineyards behind and were soon in the forest. The fir trees advanced toward them, endless columns in the light. The street was narrow and in need of repair. Every once in a while a branch slapped against the windows. To their right, the cliffs dropped off precipitously. Tschanz drove so slowly that they could hear the sound of rushing water far below.

"The Twann River gorge," Tschanz explained. "On the other side is the road to Twann."

On and off, on their left, white cliffs flashed into view, rising steeply into the night. For the rest, it was very dark, since the moon was still new. Now the road leveled out and the stream was gurgling beside them. They turned left and drove over a bridge. Before them lay a highway—the road from Twann to Lamboing. Tschanz stopped the car.

He turned off the headlights. They were in complete darkness.

"Now what?" asked Barlach.

"Now we'll wait. It's twenty to eight."

5

As they sat there waiting and it turned eight o'clock without anything happening, Barlach said it was time he learned what precisely Tschanz had in mind.

"Nothing precise, Inspector. I haven't gotten that far in the Schmied case, and you're groping in the dark too, even though you have a hunch. Right now I'm staking everything on the possibility that there'll be another party at the same house Schmied went to on Wednesday, and that a few people will come driving past on their way there. A black-tie party nowadays is bound to be a sizable affair. Of course that's just an assumption, Inspector Barlach, but in our profession, that's what assumptions are for: we test them."

The inspector interrupted his subordinate's train of thought with a skeptical objection. "The police in Biel, Neuenstadt, Twann, and Lamlingen have looked into this question of why Schmied came to this area. All their investigations have turned up nothing at all."

"Obviously Schmied's killer was smarter than the police in Biel and Neuenstadt," Tschanz said.

"How would you know that?" Barlach muttered.

"I don't suspect anyone in particular," Tschanz said. "But I do feel respect for whoever it is that killed Schmied. If I may use such a word in this connection."

Barlach listened without moving, his shoulders slightly hunched.

"And you think you'll catch this man, Tschanz, for whom you feel such respect?"

"I hope so, Inspector."

They sat in silence again and waited. Then a glow appeared in the woods near Twann. A pair of headlights glared at them. A car drove past in the direction of Lamboing and vanished into the night.

Tschanz started the motor. Two other cars passed, large dark limousines full of people. Tschanz followed them.

The woods came to an end. They drove past a restaurant with a sign that stood in the light of an open doorway, past farm houses, the glow of the last car's taillight always before them.

They reached the wide plain of the Tessenberg. The sky was swept clean, and huge presences stood in the blackness: Vega descending, Capella rising, Aldebaran, Jupiter's radiant flame.

The road turned north, they saw the outlines of mountains, the Spitzberg, the Chasseral, at their feet a few flickering lights. Those were the villages of Lamboing, Diesse, and Noids.

At that moment the cars ahead of them turned left into a dirt road, and Tschanz stopped. He rolled down his window to stick his head out. They could see the dim contours of a house standing in a field, framed by poplars, its doorway lit up, the three cars stopping in front of it. The sound of voices reached them, then everyone poured into the house and all was still. The light in the doorway went out. "They're not expecting anyone else," Tschanz said.

Barlach got out and breathed the cold night air. It felt good. He watched Tschanz park the car halfway onto the right shoulder of the road, for the street to Lamboing was narrow. Now Tschanz got out and joined the inspector. They walked down the dirt road toward the house on the field. The ground was loamy and puddles had gathered, for it had rained here too.

Then they came to a low wall with a tall, rusty iron gate set into it. The gate was closed. They looked at the house across the wall. The garden was bare, and the limousines lay among the poplars like large animals; there were no lights to be seen. Everything made a desolate impression.

It took them a while before they made out a sign attached to the middle of the gate; it was hanging at an angle. Tschanz turned on the flashlight he had brought from the car: on the sign was a capital G.

They stood in the dark again. "You see," Tschanz said, "my assumption was right. A shot in the dark, and I hit the bull's eye." And then, satisfied:

"How about a cigar, Inspector? I think I deserve one."

Barlach offered him one. "Now all we need to find out is what G stands for."

"That's no problem: Gastmann."

"How so?"

"I looked it up in the telephone book. There are only two G's in Lamboing."

Barlach let out a startled laugh, but then he said:

"Couldn't it be the other G?"

"No, that's the Gendarmerie. Or do you think a gendarme had something to do with the murder?"

"Everything's possible, Tschanz," replied the old man.

And Tschanz struck a match, but in the strong wind that was suddenly shaking the poplars as if in a rage, he found it difficult to light his cigar.

6

"I cannot understand," Barlach said, "how the police of Lamboing, Diesse, and Lignières managed to overlook this Gastmann. His house isn't exactly hidden, it's easily visible from Lamboing, in fact it would be impossible to hold a large party here without the whole village knowing about it."

Tschanz replied that he could not explain this yet either.

Thereupon they decided to walk around the house. They separated; each took a different side.

Tschanz vanished into the night and Barlach was alone. He went to the right. He turned up the collar of his coat, for it was cold. One again he felt the heavy pressure on his stomach, the violent stabs of pain, and there was a cold sweat on his forehead. He walked along the wall and followed its turn to the left. The house still lay in complete blackness.

He stopped and leaned against the wall. He saw the lights of Lamboing by the edge of the forest. Then he walked on. Again the wall changed direction, this time toward the west. The back of the house was lit up, and bright light poured through a row of windows on the second floor. He heard the sound of a piano, and when he listened more closely, he noticed that someone was playing Bach.

He walked on. According to his calculations he was about to meet

Tschanz. He strenuously peered across the brightly lit lawn, and realized too late that a dog was standing a few steps away from him.

Barlach knew a lot about dogs, but he had never seen one this size before. Though he could distinguish no details but only recognized the silhouette set off against the lighter surface of the lawn, the beast seemed to be of such terrifying proportions that Barlach instinctively froze. He saw the massive head turn slowly, as if accidentally, and stare at him. Its round eyes were bright, empty disks.

The unexpectedness of the encounter, the massive size of the animal, and the strangeness of its appearance paralyzed him. He retained the coolness of his reason, but he forgot the need for action. He looked at the beast, unafraid but captivated. This was how evil had always drawn him into its spell, the great riddle that lured him again and again to attempt a solution.

And as the dog suddenly leaped at him, a monstrous shadow hurtling through the air, a creature of pure raving murderous power, tearing him to the ground with such speed that he barely had time to raise his left arm to protect his throat, the old man did not utter a cry or so much as a sound, so natural did it all seem to him and in keeping with the laws of this world.

But just before the beast could crush the arm it had gripped with its fangs, Barlach heard the whipcrack of a shot; the body on top of him jerked, and warm blood poured onto his hand. The dog was dead.

The weight of the inert body pressed down on him, and Barlach stroked it with his hand, feeling a smooth and sweaty hide. Trembling and with an effort, he stood up, wiped his hand on the sparse grass. Tschanz came up to him, tucking the revolver back in his coat pocket as he approached.

"Are you all right, Inspector?" he asked, looking with concern at Barlach's torn sleeve.

"Absolutely. He didn't have time to bite through."

Tschanz crouched down and turned the animal's head toward the light, which was refracted in the dead eyes.

"Fangs like a wolf," he said, with a shiver. "He would have torn you to pieces, Inspector."

"You saved my life, Tschanz."

"Don't you ever carry a gun, sir?"

Barlach touched the motionless mass with his foot. "Very rarely, Tschanz," he replied, and they fell silent.

The dead dog lay on the bare, dirty ground, and they looked down at it. At their feet, a large black pool had formed—it was the blood flowing from the beast's throat like a dark lava stream.

When they looked up again, the scene had changed. The music had stopped, the lighted windows had been thrown open, and people in evening clothes were leaning out. Barlach and Tschanz looked at each other, embarrassed at finding themselves arraigned before a tribunal, as it were, and in this godforsaken spot of all places—where the fox and the hare bid each other good night, as the inspector said to himself in his annoyance.

In the middle one of the five windows stood a single man, separate from the others, who called out in a strange and clear voice, asking what they were doing down there.

"Police," Barlach replied quietly, adding that they needed to speak to Herr Gastmann.

The man replied that he thought it peculiar that they should have to kill a dog in order to meet Herr Gastmann; and besides, he was in the mood to listen to Bach. Whereupon he shut the window again, with a motion that was like his manner of speaking: unhurried, deliberate, and supremely indifferent.

A flurry of exclamations came from the windows: "Disgraceful!" "What do you think, Herr Direktor?" "Scandalous," "Unbelievable, the way the police carry on." Then the people withdrew, one window after another was shut, and all was quiet.

The two policemen had no choice but to retrace their steps. At the entrance gate, on the front side of the garden wall, a solitary figure was pacing back and forth in great agitation.

"Quick, flash your light on him," Barlach whispered at Tschanz, and in the beam of the flashlight they saw above an elegant suit and tie a rather bloated face, with features that were not undistinguished but blunted by dissipation. A heavy ring glittered on one of his hands. Upon a whispered word from Barlach, the light was switched off again.

"Who in the hell are you, fellow?" the fat man growled.

"Inspector Barlach—are you Herr Gastmann?"

"State Councillor von Schwendi, fellow, also known as Colonel von Schwendi. Good God in heaven, who do you think you are, banging around like that?"

"We are conducting an investigation and need to speak to Herr Gastmann, State Councillor," Barlach replied calmly.

The state councillor refused to be so easily appeased. "You're a separatist, aren't you?" he thundered.

Barlach decided to address him by his other title and cautiously suggested that the colonel was mistaken, this had nothing to do with the Jura problem.

But before Barlach could continue, the colonel became even more incensed than the state councillor. "So you're a communist! To hell with the lot of you! We're having a private concert here, so take your target practice somewhere else! As a colonel, I will not put up with any demonstrations against Western civilization! I will have order restored, with the Swiss Army if need be!"

Since the state councillor was evidently confused, Barlach was forced to enlighten him.

"Tschanz, don't put the state councillor's remarks in your report," he said in a dryly officious tone.

The state councillor instantly regained his composure.

"What sort of report, fellow?"

As inspector of the Criminal Investigation Department of the Bern Police, Barlach explained, he had to conduct an investigation of the murder of Police Lieutenant Schmied. It was his duty, he said, to keep a record of everything that certain persons may have to say in reply to his questions, but since . . .—and again he hesitated, unsure which of the man's two titles to use—since the colonel had evidently misconstrued the situation, he would not record the state councillor's words in his report.

The colonel was taken aback.

"So you're with the police," he said. "That's another matter."

He begged their pardon. He had an awfully full day behind him, lunch at the Turkish embassy, in the afternoon he had been elected president of an officers' club, the "Swiss Swords," then he had to attend a celebration of his election at the Helvetian Society, and earlier in the morning a special meeting of his political party, and now this get-together at Gastmann's to hear a pianist, a world-famous one, true, but still, he was dead tired.

"Isn't it possible to speak to Herr Gastmann?" Barlach asked again.

"What do you want of Gastmann?" von Schwendi replied. "What does he have to do with a murdered police lieutenant?"

"Schmied visited him last Wednesday and was killed on his way home near Twann."

"That's what you get," the state councillor said. "Gastmann invites anyone and everyone, no wonder it ends up with an incident."

Then he fell silent and appeared to be thinking.

"I am Gastmann's lawyer," he finally said. "Why did you come on this particular night? You could have at least called beforehand."

Barlach explained that he and his colleague had only just discovered Gastmann's part in the case.

The colonel was still not satisfied.

"And what about the dog?"

"He attacked me, and Tschanz had to shoot."

"Well, that's all right then," von Schwendi said, not without friendliness. "You really can't speak to Gastmann tonight. Even the police occasionally have to respect other people's social obligations. I'll have a quick word with Gastmann tonight, and I'll be in your office tomorrow. Do you happen to have a picture of Schmied?"

Barlach took a photograph from his wallet and gave it to him.

"Thank you," the state councillor said.

Then he nodded and went inside.

Now Barlach and Tschanz walked back to where they had stood earlier, in front of the rusty bars of the garden gate; the front of the house was still dark.

"You can't get past a state councillor," Barlach said, "and if he's a colonel and a lawyer on top of it, he's got three devils inside him at once. So here we are with our lovely murder, and there's nothing we can do."

Tschanz was silent and seemed to pondering something. Finally he said, "It is nine o'clock, Inspector. I think the best thing we can do is look up the policeman of Lamboing and find out what he knows about Gastmann."

"Right," Barlach said. "You can do that. Try to find out why no one in Lamboing knows anything about Schmied's visiting Gastmann. I'm going to that little restaurant at the edge of the gorge. I have to do something for my stomach. I'll expect you there."

They walked back along the path to the car. Tschanz drove off and reached Lamboing after a few minutes.

He found the policeman in the inn, together with Clenin, who had come up from Twann. They were sitting at a table apart from the farmers. Evidently they had something private to discuss. The policeman of Lamboing was short, fat, and red-haired. His name was Jean Pierre Charnel.

Tschanz joined them, and soon the suspicion the two men felt for their colleague from Bern was dissipated, although Charnel minded having to switch from French to German, a language in which he felt himself on slippery ground. They were drinking white wine, and Tschanz ate some bread and cheese with it. He did not mention that he had just come from Gastmann's house, but asked instead if they still had not found any clues.

"*Non,*" said Charnel, "not a trace of *assassin*. *On a rien trouvé,* nothing was found."

Charnel went on to say that in this area there was only one person worth questioning, a Herr Gastmann, the one who had bought Rollier's house, where there were always a lot of guests, and on Wednesday he'd had a big party. But Schmied hadn't been there, Gastmann didn't even know his name. "*Schmied n'etait pas chez Gastmann, impossible.* Completely impossible."

Tschanz listened to the man's garbled talk and suggested questioning some other people who had been at Gastmann's on that day.

"I've done that," Clenin interjected. "There's a writer in Schernelz, above Ligerz, who knows Gastmann well and visits him often. He says he was there on Wednesday. He doesn't know anything about Schmied, never heard his name, and he doesn't believe Gastmann ever had a policeman in his house."

"A writer, you say?" Tschanz frowned. "I'll have to buttonhole that one some time. Writers are a two-faced bunch, but I know how to handle a smart-ass."

"So tell me, Charnel," he continued, "who is this Gastmann?"

"*Un monsieur très riche,*" the policeman of Lamboing replied enthusiastically. "Has money like hay and *très noble.* He give tip to my *fiancée*"—and he pointed proudly at the waitress—"*comme un roi,* but not on purpose to have something with her. *Jamais.*"

"What's his profession?"

"*Philosophe.*"

"What does that mean to you, Charnel?"

"A man who think much and do nothing."

"But he must make money somehow?"

Charnel shook his head. "He do not make money, he have money. He pay taxes for the whole village of Lamboing. That is enough for us to make Gastmann the man most *sympathique* in the whole canton."

"We'll still have to have a close look at this Gastmann. I'm going to see him tomorrow."

"Watch out for his dog," Charnel warned. "*Un chien tres dangereux.*"

Tschanz stood up and patted the policeman of Lamboing on the shoulder. "Don't worry, I can handle his dog."

7

It was ten o'clock when Tschanz left Clenin and Charnel to join Barlach in the restaurant by the ravine. But when he came to the spot where the dirt road branched off to Gastmann's house, he stopped his car. He got out and slowly walked to the garden gate and then along the wall. The house still looked dark and solitary, surrounded by giant poplars swaying in the wind. The limousines were still parked in the garden. Tschanz did not go all the way around the house, but stopped at a corner from which he could survey the lighted windows in the back. Now and then the shapes of people were silhouetted against the yellow panes, and Tschanz pressed himself close to the wall to avoid being seen. He scanned the sparse patch of lawn where the dog had lain. It was no longer there. Someone must have removed it. Only the black pool of blood still glinted in the light from the windows. Tschanz returned to the car.

Barlach was not in the restaurant when he got there. The proprietress said he had left for Twann half an hour ago, after drinking a brandy—he hadn't stayed more than five minutes.

Tschanz wondered what the old man was up to, but he was unable to pursue his speculations; the narrow road demanded all his attention. He drove past the bridge where they had waited, and drove on into the forest.

And now something strange and uncanny occurred that put him

in a pensive mood. He had been driving quickly when suddenly the lake flashed into view from below, a nocturnal mirror framed by white cliffs. He realized he had reached the scene of the murder. At that moment, a dark figure detached itself from the wall of rock and clearly signaled for the car to stop.

Tschanz halted automatically and opened the right-hand door of the car. He regretted this immediately, for he realized that he was going through precisely the same motions Schmied had just moments before he was shot. He thrust his hand in his coat pocket and gripped his revolver. The touch of its cool steel calmed him. The figure came closer. Then he recognized who it was: Barlach. But far from relieving him, this realization filled him with a hot, secret terror that he could not explain to himself. Barlach stooped and they looked each other in the face—for hours, it seemed, though it was only a few seconds. Neither of them said a word, and their eyes were like stones. Then Barlach got into the car, and Tschanz released his grip on the gun in his pocket.

"You can drive on, Tschanz," Barlach said, and his voice sounded indifferent. But Tschanz noticed with a start that the old man had addressed him with "*du*" instead of the formal "*Sie.*" From then on, the inspector persisted in this more intimate form of address.

Not until they passed Biel did Barlach break the silence and ask what Tschanz had experienced in Lamboing, "and let's settle once and for all on calling the place by its French name."

When Tschanz told him that both Charnel and Clenin thought it impossible that Schmied had been a guest at Gastmann's, Barlach said nothing; and as for the writer from Schernelz whom Clenin had mentioned, Barlach said he would speak to the man himself.

Tschanz spoke with more animation than usual. He was relieved that they were talking at all, and he wanted to drown out the strange agitation he felt, but before they reached Schupfen, they were both silent again.

Shortly after eleven, they stopped in front of Barlach's house, and the inspector got out.

"Thanks again, Tschanz," he said, and shook his hand. "It's an embarrassing thing to talk about: but the fact is, you saved my life."

He stood on the pavement and followed the vanishing taillight of the speeding car. "Now he can drive as fast he likes."

He entered his house by the unlocked door. In the book-lined hallway he put his hand in his coat pocket and pulled out a weapon, which he carefully placed on the desk next to the snake. It was a large, heavy revolver.

Then he slowly took off his overcoat. Wrapped around his left arm was a thick cloth bandage, the kind animal trainers use to teach a dog to attack.

8

The next morning, the old inspector knew from experience that some "unpleasantness"—his word for friction with Lutz—was to be expected. "You know what Saturdays are like," he told himself as he crossed the Altenberg bridge. "That's when the bureaucrats bare their teeth just because they're ashamed of not having done anything sensible the whole week." He was dressed in solemn black, for Schmied's funeral was scheduled for ten o'clock. There was no way he could avoid attending it, and that was the real source of his irritation.

Von Schwendi appeared at police headquarters shortly after eight, bypassing Barlach and instead going to Lutz, who had just received Tschanz's report about the previous night's events.

Von Schwendi was in the same political faction as Lutz, the conservative liberal-socialist wing of the Independent Party. He had actively lobbied for Lutz's advancement, and ever since a tête-à-tête over dinner following a closed session of the executive committee, Lutz and von Schwendi had been on "*du*" terms, even though Lutz had not been elected to the local parliament seat; for in Bern, as von Schwendi explained, it is practically impossible for a man with the first name of Lucius to become a people's representative.

"It's really something," he began the moment his bulky shape appeared in the doorway, "the way your people from the Bern police carry on, my dear Lutz. They shoot my client Gastmann's dog, a rare South American breed, and disrupt culture—Anatol Kraushaar-Raffaeli, a world-famous pianist. Let's face it: the Swiss have no education, no cosmopolitan character, not a trace of European consciousness. There's only one remedy: three years of military service."

Lutz, who found the visit of his political associate embarrassing, and who was afraid of his endless tirades, offered von Schwendi a seat.

"We are embroiled in an extremely difficult investigation," he said, intimidated. "You know it yourself, and the young policeman who is conducting it for the main part is, by Swiss standards, rather good at his job. The old inspector who was with him is, admittedly, somewhat rusty. I regret the death of such a rare South American dog. I'm an animal lover and own a dog myself, and I will order a special, thorough investigation. Our men just haven't the faintest inkling of real criminology. When I think of Chicago, I find our situation downright hopeless."

Lutz paused, unsettled by von Schwendi's unblinking stare, and by the time he resumed speaking, he felt profoundly unsure of himself.

"I would like to know," he said, "whether the murdered man, Schmied, was a guest at your client's house last Wednesday evening. You see, we have some reason to believe that he was."

"My dear Lutz," the colonel replied, "let's not play games here. You people know all about Schmied's visits to Gastmann, you can't fool me."

"What do you mean by that, State Councillor?" In his bewilderment, Lutz reverted to the formal address. He had never felt quite at ease conversing with von Schwendi on a "*du*" basis.

The lawyer leaned back, folded his hands in front of his chest, and bared his teeth, a pose that had contributed substantially to his attaining his colonel's rank as well as his state councillor's title.

"My dear doctor," he said, "I'd really like to know once and for all why you people had this Schmied fellow sniffing around good old Gastmann. Because whatever is going on out there in the Jura Mountains, it's none of the police's damn business, we don't have a Gestapo here, not yet at any rate."

Lutz was flabbergasted. "Why on earth would we have Schmied investigate your client, who is completely unknown to us?" he asked helplessly. "And why should a murder be none of our business?"

"If you don't know that Schmied attended Gastmann's parties in Lamboing under the name of Doctor Prantl, lecturer on American Cultural History in Münich, then the entire police force should resign for reasons of total incompetence." Agitated, von Schwendi drummed his fingers on Lutz's desk.

"My dear Oscar, we don't know anything about it," Lutz said, relieved to have finally remembered the state councillor's first name. "What you are telling me is real news to me."

"Aha," von Schwendi said dryly, and lapsed into silence. Lutz was becoming more and more conscious of his inferiority. Sensing that he would have to yield step by step to whatever the colonel might require of him, he helplessly glanced at the Traffelets on the wall, at the marching soldiers, the fluttering Swiss flags, the general on his horse. The state councillor noted the police chief's embarrassment with satisfaction and decided to clarify the caustic meaning of his "Aha."

"So it's news to the police," he said. "Once again the police know nothing at all."

Even though confessing it was extremely unpleasant, and though von Schwendi's bullying was very nearly intolerable, the police chief was forced to admit that Schmied had not visited Gastmann on official assignment, that the police had in fact been ignorant of his trips to Lamboing. "Evidently," he said, "Schmied was acting purely on his own. As for why he would assume a false name—I cannot at present explain this either."

Von Schwendi bent forward and fixed his bloodshot, watery eyes on Lutz. "That explains everything," he said. "Schmied was spying for a foreign power."

"What do you mean?" By now Lutz was floundering more than ever.

"What I mean," said the state councillor, "is that the police must find out Schmied's motives for visiting Gastmann."

"The police, my dear Oscar, should first and above all find out some things about Gastmann," said Lutz.

"Gastmann is no threat to the police," von Schwendi retorted, "and besides I don't want you or anyone from the police to concern yourselves with him. That is his wish, he is my client, and it's my duty to see that his wishes are complied with."

This insolent reply had such a shattering effect on Lutz that at first he was unable to formulate a response. He lit a cigarette, forgetting in his confusion to offer one to von Schwendi. Then he finally shifted his position in his chair and replied:

"Unfortunately, the fact that Schmied visited Gastmann forces us to concern ourselves with your client, my dear Oscar."

Von Schwendi would not be deterred. "Not so much with my client," he said, "but mainly with me, since I am Gastmann's lawyer. It's your good fortune, Lutz, that you have me to deal with, because frankly, I want to help you as well as Gastmann. Naturally, the whole case is disagreeable for my client, but I dare say it's even more embarrassing for you, since the police are still groping in the dark. And frankly, I doubt whether you'll ever be able to cast any light on this affair."

"The police," Lutz replied, "have solved almost every murder, that is a statistically proven fact. I admit that in the Schmied case we've run into certain difficulties, but we have also"—he hesitated for a moment—"arrived at some remarkable results. It's we, after all, who discovered the Gastmann connection, and it's again because of our actions that Gastmann has sent you to us. It's up to Gastmann now to explain his connection to Schmied, it's his problem, not ours. Schmied was in his house, under a false identity, true, but that is precisely the reason why the police are obliged to concern themselves with Gastmann, for surely the murdered man's peculiar behavior does implicate Gastmann. We must have a talk with Gastmann. Unless, of course, you can furnish a satisfactory explanation as to why Schmied visited your client under a false name, not just once but several times, according to our findings."

"All right," von Schwendi said. "Let's get down to brass tacks. You will see in due course that it's you and not I who will have to furnish a satisfactory explanation as to what Gastmann was after in Lamboing. It's you, the police, who are in the dock here, not we, my dear Lutz."

With these words he pulled out of his briefcase a large white sheet of paper, unfolded it, and laid it on the police chief's desk.

"These are the names of the persons who have been guests at Gastmann's house," he said. "The list is complete. I have divided it into three sections. The first we'll ignore, it's irrelevant, those are the artists. No offense against Kraushaar-Raffaeli, he's a foreigner; no, I mean the local types, the ones from Utzendorf and Merlingen. They either write plays about Niklaus Manuel and the battle of Morgarten or else it's one mountain landscape after another. The second section are the industrialists. You'll see the names, they have a proud ring to them, these are men whom I regard as the finest representatives of Swiss society. I say this quite openly, even though I myself come from peasant stock on my maternal grandmother's side."

"And the third section?" asked Lutz, since the state councillor had suddenly stopped talking. Von Schwendi's calm made the police chief nervous, which of course was his intention.

"The third section," von Schwendi finally continued, "makes the Schmied affair unpleasant for you and also, I have to admit this, for the industrialists; because now I am compelled to disclose certain matters that should really be kept secret from the police. But since you people couldn't resist tracking down Gastmann and digging up the embarrassing fact that Schmied was in Lamboing, the industrialists now find themselves forced to instruct me to give the police as many details as the investigation of the Schmied case may require. The unpleasantness for us consists in having to divulge political matters of eminent importance, and the unpleasantness for you is that your authority as policemen extends to all Swiss and foreign nationals in this country *except* for the ones listed in section three."

"I don't understand a word of what you're saying," Lutz said.

"You've never understood a thing about politics, my dear Lucius," von Schwendi replied. "The third section contains the names of members of a foreign embassy. That embassy does not want to be mentioned in association with a certain class of industrialists."

9

Now Lutz understood the state councillor, and there was a long silence in the police chief's room. The telephone rang, and Lutz lifted the receiver only to shout the word "Conference!" into it, after which he fell silent again. At long last he spoke:

"But as far as I know, our government is now officially negotiating a new trade agreement with this same foreign power."

"That's absolutely true, negotiations are under way," the colonel replied. "Official negotiations—why not, the diplomats want to have something to do. But there are also unofficial negotiations, and in Lamboing, the negotiations are private. Modern industry, my dear Lutz, involves negotiations in which the state may not and must not interfere."

"Of course," Lutz agreed, thoroughly intimidated.

"Of course," von Schwendi repeated. "And as we now both know, the unfortunately murdered police lieutenant Ulrich Schmied secretly attended these meetings under a false name."

The police chief sat as if stunned, and von Schwendi saw that his calculation was paying off. Lutz was now so deflated that the state councillor would be able to do with him as he wished. As is frequently the case with determined and simpleminded natures, this earnest official was so upset by the unexpected developments in the Schmied murder case that he allowed himself to be influenced and made concessions that a more objective reflection would have counseled him against. To spare himself further humiliation, he tried to make light of his predicament.

"Dear Oscar," he said, "it doesn't look all that grave to me. Of course Swiss industrialists have a right to negotiate privately with whoever is interested, even with that foreign power. I would never dispute that, nor do the police interfere in these matters. I repeat, Schmied went to Gastmann on his own initiative, and I want to officially apologize for that; it was certainly irregular for him to hide behind an assumed name and pretend to have another profession, although, being a policeman myself, I can understand why he might have felt inhibited in that company. But he wasn't the only one there. What about all those artists, my dear State Councillor?"

"Decoration. We live in a cultured society, Lutz, and we need to advertise that. The negotiations have to be kept secret, and artists are good for that. Everyone dining together, a nice roast, wine, cigars, women, conversation, the artists get bored, huddle in little groups, drink, and never notice that the capitalists and the representatives of that foreign power are sitting together. They don't want to notice, because they're not interested. Artists are only interested in art. But a policeman sitting there can find out everything. No, Lutz, there's something very dubious about this Schmied of yours."

"I'm sorry, but I can only repeat that as yet, we have no clue as to why Schmied visited Gastmann."

"If the police didn't send him, someone else did," replied von Schwendi. "There are foreign powers, dear Lucius, that are interested in what's going on in Lamboing. I'm talking about world politics."

"Schmied was not a spy."

"We have every reason to suspect that he was one. It is better for Switzerland's honor if he was a spy than if he was a police agent."

"Now he is dead," sighed the police chief, who would have given anything to be able to ask Schmied himself.

"That's not our concern," said the colonel. "I don't want to cast suspicion on anyone, but the fact is that the only conceivable party interested in keeping the negotiations in Lamboing secret is that foreign power. For us, it's a question of money; for them, it's political principle. Let's not deceive ourselves. But if Schmied's death is their doing, the police will be rather severely handicapped."

Lutz stood up and went to the window. "I still don't quite see how your client Gastmann fits into this picture," he said, speaking slowly.

Von Schwendi fanned himself with the large sheet of paper and replied, "Gastmann put his house at the disposal of the industrialists and diplomats attending those meetings."

"But why Gastmann?"

"My highly respected client," growled the colonel, "was a man of the requisite caliber. As a former Argentine ambassador to China, he enjoyed the trust of the foreign power, and as former chief of the tin syndicate, he had the confidence of the industrialists. And besides, he lived in Lamboing."

"How do you mean, Oscar?"

Von Schwendi smiled. "Did you ever hear of Lamboing before Schmied was murdered?"

"No."

"That's just it," said the state councillor. "No one has ever heard of Lamboing, and we needed an obscure site for our meetings. So you may as well leave Gastmann alone. I'm sure you can understand that he doesn't relish close contact with the police, that he doesn't appreciate your sniffing and prying, your endless questions. You can do that with your common crooks and gangsters, but not with a man who refused to be inducted into the French Academy. And besides, the men you sent out there couldn't have been more clumsy if they tried. You don't shoot a dog during a Bach recital. Not that Gastmann is insulted. He's completely indifferent. If your men machine-gunned his house he wouldn't raise an eyebrow. It's just that there's no sense in bothering him any longer, since the forces behind this murder have nothing to do with our decent Swiss industrialists or with Gastmann."

The police chief paced back and forth in front of the window. "We will now have to focus our investigation on Schmied's life," he said. "As for that foreign power, we will make a report to the attorney general. To what extent he will want to take over the case I can't say yet, but he will leave most of the job to us. I will comply with your request that we spare Gastmann any unnecessary inconvenience; we certainly won't search his house. However, if I should need to speak to him, I must ask you to arrange a meeting at which you would be present. That way Gastmann and I could dispose of the necessary formalities in a relaxed and casual way. I'm not talking about a formal inquest but about a formality within the framework of the inquest, since, under certain conditions, the inquest may require that we interrogate Gastmann, meaningless though that may be; but an inquest has to be complete. We'll talk about art, that'll keep the procedure as innocuous as possible, and I won't ask any questions. If I should be forced to ask a question—for formal reasons—I would let you know that question in advance."

By now, the state councillor had also risen to his feet, and the two men stood facing each other. The state councillor tapped the police chief on the shoulder.

"So we're in agreement," he said. "You will leave Gastmann alone, my dear little Lucius, I'm holding you to that. I'll leave the list with you: it's accurate and complete. I've been busy telephoning all night, everyone's very upset. No one knows whether the foreign embassy will want to continue negotiating once they learn about the Schmied case. Millions are at stake, doctor: millions! I wish you luck with your investigation. You'll need it."

With these words von Schwendi stomped out of the room.

10

Lutz had just enough time to glance through the state councillor's list, a roster of some of the nation's most illustrious names, and lower it again with a groan—good God, he thought, how did I ever get myself involved in this—when Barlach stepped in, without knocking, as usual. The old man had come to ask for authorization to interrogate Gastmann in Lamboing, but Lutz put him off until the afternoon. "It's time to go to the funeral," he said, and stood up.

Barlach did not object, and left the room with Lutz, who was beginning to regret his foolhardy promise to leave Gastmann alone. He was also beginning to fear Barlach's opinion, which was not likely to be sympathetic. They stood on the street, both of them silent, both of them dressed in black coats with turned-up collars. It was raining, but since it was just a few steps to the car, they didn't open their umbrellas. Blatter was driving. The moment they took off, the clouds burst and the rain came down in violent cascades that were driven slantwise against the car windows. Lutz and Barlach sat motionless, each in his own corner. Now I have to tell him, thought Lutz, looking at Barlach's calm profile. The inspector put his hand on his stomach.

"Are you in pain?" Lutz asked.

"Always," Barlach replied.

Then they fell silent again, and Lutz thought, I'll tell him in the afternoon. Blatter drove slowly. The downpour was so heavy that everything around them vanished behind a white wall. Somewhere, streetcars and automobiles swam about in these monstrous falling seas. Lutz did not know where they were, the dripping windows permitted no view. It was getting darker in the car. Lutz lit a cigarette, exhaled, decided to avoid any discussion of Gastmann with the old man, and said:

"The newspapers will report the murder, there was no way to keep it secret."

"There's no need to any more," Barlach said, "now that we've found a clue."

Lutz extinguished his cigarette. "There never was any need."

Barlach said nothing, and Lutz, who would have welcomed an argument, peered through the window again. The rain had begun to subside. They had already reached the avenue leading to Schlosshalden Cemetery, the gray, rain-soaked walls were pushing into view behind steaming tree trunks. Blatter drove into the courtyard and stopped. They got out of the car, opened their umbrellas, and walked through the rows of graves. They did not have to search for long. The gravestones and crosses receded, it seemed they had entered a construction site. The earth was riddled with freshly dug graves, and each grave was covered with planks. The moisture from the wet grass penetrated their mud-caked shoes. In the middle of this cleared space, surrounded by all those still tenantless graves, at the bottom of which the rain had collected in dirty puddles, among improvised wooden crosses and mounds of earth covered with heaps of rapidly rotting flowers and wreaths, a group of people was standing around a grave. The coffin had not been lowered yet. The priest was reading from the bible. Beside him, shivering in a ludicrous work suit that resembled a frock coat, holding up an umbrella for both the priest and himself, the gravedigger was shifting his weight from one foot to the other. Barlach and Lutz stopped next to the grave. The older man heard someone crying. It was Frau Schönler's rotund, shapeless form in the ceaseless rain, and next to her stood Tschanz, without an umbrella, in a coat with the collar turned up and the belt hanging loose, a stiff black hat on his head. Next to him a girl, pale, hatless, blond hair dripping down in long strands. It occurred to Barlach that this must be Anna. Tschanz bowed, Lutz nodded, the inspector stood motionless and impassive. He looked across at the others standing around the grave, policemen, all of them, all of them out of uniform, all wearing the same raincoats, the same stiff black hats, holding their umbrellas like sabers, a group of sentries blown in from some unearthly place to watch over the dead, unreal in their earnestness. And behind them, hastily summoned from all over town and assembled in serried ranks, the municipal band in their black and red uniforms, desperately trying to protect their yellow instruments under their coats. And so they all stood around the coffin, a wooden box without a wreath, without flowers, but nevertheless the only warm and sheltering thing in this relentlessly regular pouring and dripping without foreseeable end. The priest had stopped talking a long time ago. No one noticed. There was only the rain, nothing else existed. The priest coughed. Once. Then several times. Thereupon the bassoons, French horns, cornets, trombones, and tubas blared forth in a proud and stately wail, yellow flashes of light in the floods of rain; but then they, too, subsided, faltered, gave up. Everyone crept back under umbrellas and coats. The rain was falling more and more strongly, shoes sank into the mud, rivers flowed into the empty grave. Lutz bowed and stepped forward. He looked at the wet coffin and bowed again.

"Men," he said somewhere in the rain, almost inaudible through the veils of water, "Men, our comrade Schmied is no more."

Suddenly he was interrupted by a wild, raucous song:

"The devil goes round,
   the devil goes round,
   he beats the people into the ground!"

Two men in black frock coats came staggering across the cemetery. Without umbrellas or overcoats, they were at the mercy of the rain. Their clothes clung to their limbs. Both wore top hats from which water streamed into their faces. They were carrying an enormous laurel wreath with a ribbon that trailed in the mud. They were huge, brutal men, butchers in evening wear, drunk to the gills, constantly on the verge of keeling over, but since they never stumbled at the same time, each of them managed to hold himself up by the laurel wreath that rose and fell between them like a ship in distress. Now they launched into a new song:

> "The miller's wife, 'er 'usband is dead,
> And she is alive, alive,
> She married the miller's apprentice instead,
> And she is alive, alive."

They ran up to the group of mourners and threw themselves into their midst, right between Frau Schönler and Tschanz. No one hindered them, everyone stood as if petrified, and already they were staggering off through the wet grass, leaning upon and clinging to each other, falling over grave mounds, knocking down crosses. Their singsong died away in the rain, and everything was covered up again.

> "Everything passes,
> everything goes!"

was the last that was heard of them. Only the wreath remained. They had dropped it onto the coffin. Written in running black letters on the muddied ribbon were the words: "To our dear Dr. Prantl."

But just as the people around the grave had recovered from their shock and were about to voice their indignation, and as the municipal band burst into another desperate wail in an effort to reclaim the solemnity of the occasion, the wind and the rain started whipping about with such rampant fury that everyone fled, leaving only the gravediggers, black scarecrows in the howling torrent, to finally lower the coffin into the grave.

11

When Barlach was back in the car with his boss, and Blatter was weaving his way through fleeing policemen and musicians, Lutz finally gave vent to his anger:

"Unbelievable, this Gastmann!"

"I don't understand," the old man said.

"Schmied frequented Gastmann's house under the name of Prantl."

"In that case we've been given a warning," Barlach replied, but asked nothing further. They were driving toward Muristalden, where Lutz lived. This is the right moment, Lutz thought. Now I'll tell the old man about Gastmann, and why he must be left alone. But again he remained silent. He got out at the Burgernziel, leaving Barlach in the car.

"Shall I drive you into the city, Inspector?" asked the policeman behind the wheel.

"No, drive me home, Blatter."

Blatter drove faster now. The storm had relaxed, and suddenly, by the Muristalden, Barlach found himself steeped in blinding light: the sun broke through the clouds, disappeared, came out again, and was caught up in a rollicking chase of mists and clouds, huge bulging mounds that came racing in from the West to pile up in front of the mountains, casting wild shadows across the city that lay spread out by the river between forests and hills like a body devoid of will and resistance. Barlach's tired hand stroked his wet coat, his narrowed eyes glittered as he avidly drank in the spectacle: the world was beautiful. Blatter stopped. Barlach thanked him and got out of the car. It was no longer raining, only the wind was left, the wet, cold wind. The old man stood waiting for Blatter to turn the heavy car around, and waved once more as the policeman drove off. Then he stepped up to the edge of the Aare river. The water was high and dirty brown. A rusty old baby carriage came swimming along, branches, a small fir tree, and then, dancing, a little paper boat. Barlach watched the river for a long time, he loved it. Then he went through the garden and into the house.

Barlach changed his shoes before entering the hall. At the door to his study, he stopped. Behind the desk sat a man who was leafing through Schmied's dossier. His right hand was toying with Barlach's Turkish knife.

"So it's you," said the old man.

"Yes, it's me," said the other.

Barlach closed the door and sat down in his armchair facing the desk. Silently he watched as the other calmly turned the pages in Schmied's folder, an almost peasant-like figure, calm and withdrawn, deep-set eyes in a bony but round face, short-cropped hair.

"So you call yourself Gastmann now," the old man finally said.

The other pulled out a pipe, stuffed it without taking his eyes off Barlach, lit it, and, tapping the folder with his index finger, replied:

"You've been well aware of that for a while. It was you who set that boy at my heels. These notes are yours."

Then he closed the folder again. Barlach glanced at the desk. There was his gun, with the butt turned toward him, all he had to do was reach out. Then he said:

"I'll never stop hunting you. Some day I'll succeed in proving your crimes."

"You'll have to hurry up, Barlach," the other replied. "You don't have much time. The doctors give you another year if you let them operate on you now."

"You're right," said the old man. "One more year. And I can't let them operate now. I have to live up to this challenge. It's my last chance."

"Your last," confirmed the other, and then they both sat silently facing each other for a long time.

"It was over forty years ago that we first met," the other began again. "I'm sure you remember. It was in some tumbledown Jewish tavern in the Bosporus. There was a shapeless yellow Swiss cheese of a moon dangling between the clouds, we could see it through the rotting rafters. You, Barlach, were a young Swiss police specialist hired by the Turks to institute some sort of reform, and I—well, I was what I still am, a globetrotter, an adventurer, avid to live this one life that I have and to learn all there is to learn about this mysterious and singular planet. We loved each other at first sight, sitting there among dirty Greeks and Jews in their caftans. But when those infernal liquors we poured down our gullets, those fermented juices of God knows what sort of dates and those flaming seas from the cornfields of Odessa, when all that started boiling up inside us, making our eyes burn like glowing embers through the Turkish night, our talk started heating up. Oh, I love to think of that hour that set us both on our courses!"

He laughed.

The old man sat and watched him in silence.

"You have one more year to live," the other continued, "and for forty years you've given me a tough chase. That is the upshot. What did we talk about, Barlach, in the rot of that bar in a suburb called Tophane, swathed in Turkish cigarette smoke? Your thesis was that human imperfection—the fact that we can never predict with certainty how others will act, and that furthermore we have no way of calculating the ways chance interferes in our plans—guarantees that most crimes will perforce be detected. To commit a crime, you said, is an act of stupidity, because you can't operate with people as if they were chessmen. Against this I contended, more for the sake of argument than out of conviction, that it's precisely this incalculable, chaotic element in human relations that makes it possible to commit crimes that *cannot* be detected, and that for this reason the ma-

THE JUDGE AND HIS HANGMAN · 51

jority of crimes are not only not punished, but are simply not known, because, in effect, they are perfectly hidden.

"And as we kept arguing, seduced by those infernal fires the Jew kept pouring into our glasses, and even more by our own exuberant youth, we ended up making a bet, and it happened just as the moon was sinking behind Asia Minor, a wager which we defiantly pinned to the sky, very much like the kind of horrible joke that offends against everything sacred and yet holds out such a devilish appeal, such a wicked temptation of the spirit by the spirit, that we cannot suppress it."

"You're right," the old man calmly said, "that's when we made that bet."

"You didn't think I would go through with it," laughed the other, "the way we woke up in that desolate bar the next morning, you on a rotting bench and I under a table that was still soaked with liquor."

"I didn't think," Barlach replied, "that anyone would be capable of going through with it."

They were silent.

"Lead us not into temptation," the other began again. "You were always such a good boy, your probity was never in danger of being tempted, but I was tempted by your probity. I kept my bold vow to commit a crime in your presence without your being able to prove that I did it."

"Three days later," the old man said softly, immersed in his memories, "we were crossing the Mahmoud Bridge with a German merchant, and you pushed him into the water in front of my eyes."

"Yes, the poor fellow couldn't swim, and your own natatory skills were so modest that after your failed attempt to rescue him they had to drag you half drowned from the dirty waters of the Golden Horn," the other replied, unperturbed. "The murder took place on a brilliant Turkish summer day, with a pleasant breeze blowing in from the sea, on a crowded bridge in full view of amorous couples from the European colony, Muslims, and local beggars, and yet you could not prove my guilt. You had me arrested, in vain. Interrogations, hour after hour, useless. The court believed my version, that the merchant had committed suicide."

"You were able to prove that he was on the brink of bankruptcy and had tried, unsuccessfully, to save himself by committing a fraud," the old man admitted, bitterly, paler than usual.

"I chose my victim carefully, my friend," laughed the other.

"And so you became a criminal," said the inspector.

The other toyed absently with the Turkish knife.

"I can't very well deny that I am something like a criminal," he finally said in a casual manner. "I became better and better at it, and you got better and better at your criminology: but I was always one step ahead of you, and you have never been able to catch up. I kept looming up in your career like some gray apparition, I couldn't resist the temptation to commit crimes right under your nose, each one bolder, wilder, and more outrageous than the last, and time after time you were unable to prove them. You could defeat fools, but I defeated you."

His gaze was amused and alert as he continued: "So that's how we lived our lives. Yours was spent in humble subordination, in police stations and musty offices, climbing the ladder of your modest achievements one rung at a time, waging war against petty forgers and thieves, poor bastards who never learned to stand up straight, a couple of pathetic murderers at best, while I ran the whole gamut of life, from the deepest obscurity, lost in the thicket of desolate cities, to the spotlight of an illustrious position, covered with medals, doing good for the sheer hell of it, and when it so pleased me, committing evil and loving it. What an adventure! Your deepest desire was to ruin my life, and mine, to spite you by living my life as I did. Truly, that one night chained us together forever!"

The man behind Barlach's desk clapped his hands together, it was one single, cruel slap. "Now we've arrived at the end of our careers," he cried. "You've come back half defeated to your dear old Bern, a sleepy, innocuous town where no one can distinguish the living from the dead, and I've come back to Lamboing, this too on the spur of a whim: it's nice to round things off, because, you see, it's in this godforsaken village that some woman long since dead gave birth to me, without much thought and very little sense, which is why I stole away one rainy night when I was thirteen years old. So here we are again. Give it up, my friend, it's pointless. Death does not wait."

And now, with an almost imperceptible movement of his hand, he threw the knife. It grazed Barlach's cheek and plunged deep into the armchair. The old man did not move. The other laughed.

"So you think I killed Schmied?"

"It's my job to investigate this case," replied the inspector.

The other stood up and took the dossier.

"I'm taking this with me."

"One day I'll succeed in proving your crimes," Barlach said for the second time. "And this is my last chance."

"Inside this briefcase is the scanty evidence Schmied collected for you in Lamboing. Without it you're lost. You don't have any copies or photostats, I know you."

"No, I don't," the old man admitted.

"How about using the gun to stop me?" the other asked with a smile.

"You took out the cartridges," Barlach replied, stone faced.

"That's right," said the other, patting him on the shoulder. Then he walked past the old man, the door opened and closed, a second door opened and closed outside. Barlach was still sitting in his armchair, leaning his cheek against the cold blade of the knife. But suddenly he seized the gun and opened it. It was loaded. He jumped up, ran into the vestibule, tore open the front door, gun in hand:

The street was empty.

Then came the pain, the overwhelming, monstrous, stabbing pain, a sun rising inside him, it threw him onto the couch, convulsed him, scalded and shook him with feverish heat. The old man crawled on his hands and knees like an animal, threw himself on the ground, dragged himself across the rug, and finally lay still somewhere in his room between the chairs, covered with cold sweat. "What is man?" he moaned softly. "What is man?"

12

But he recovered. After the attack, he felt an unusual sensation: complete freedom from pain. He heated some wine and drank it in small, careful sips. That was all he ate or drank. He didn't refrain, however, from taking his customary walk though the city and across the Bundesterrasse. He was still half unconscious, but the air was so pure, as if washed by the storm, that he felt himself reviving with each step.

When Lutz saw Barlach come into his office, he noticed nothing; perhaps he was too preoccupied with his own bad conscience. He decided to tell Barlach about his talk with von Schwendi right away, instead of waiting till the end of the day. For this purpose, he assumed a cold impersonal stance, puffing out his chest like the general in Traffelet's picture above him, and briefed the old man in a clipped and curt telegram style. But to his boundless surprise, the inspector raised no objection. He was in complete agreement: pending instructions from the federal government, the investigation should be limited to an examination of Schmied's life. Lutz was so surprised that he gave up his pose and became chatty and affable.

"Naturally I've found out some things about Gastmann," he said, "and I know enough about him to be certain that he couldn't possibly be the killer."

"Of course," the old man said.

Lutz, who had received some new data from Biel during his lunch hour, put on an air of assurance.

"Born in Pockau, Saxony, son of a leather merchant. Starts out as an Argentinian—must have emigrated as a young man—, serves as Argentine ambassador to China. After that he's French, usually away on some long trip abroad. He was awarded the Cross of the Foreign Legion and is known as a scientist, published several works on questions of biology. As for his character: the man was elected to the French Academy and declined to accept the honor. I find that impressive."

"Interesting trait," Barlach said.

"We're still investigating his two servants. They have French passports, but it seems they're from the Emmental. That was a nasty joke he had them play on us at the funeral."

"That appears to be Gastmann's sense of humor," the old man said.

"He's probably upset about the death of his dog. But we have even greater cause to be upset. This whole Schmied case is putting us in a very wrong light. We can count ourselves lucky that I'm on friendly terms with von Schwendi. Gastmann is a man of international caché, and he enjoys the full confidence of Swiss industrialists."

"Then he must be all right," Barlach said.

"His character is above all suspicion."

"Definitely," the old man nodded.

"Unfortunately we can no longer say the same about Schmied." With these words, Lutz concluded the conversation. He picked up the receiver and asked the operator to connect him with the House of Parliament.

But as Lutz sat waiting with the receiver against his ear, the inspector, who had already turned to leave, stopped and said:

"I have to ask you for a week's sick leave, Dr. Lutz."

"That's quite all right," Lutz said, covering the mouthpiece with his palm, since the call was coming through. "You needn't come in on Monday."

*

Tschanz was waiting in Barlach's office. He stood up when the old man came in. He had a calm demeanor, but the inspector sensed that the policeman was nervous.

"Let's drive out to Gastmann's house," Tschanz said, "it's high time we did that."

"To the writer," the old man replied, and put on his coat.

"Detours, nothing but detours," Tschanz said angrily as he followed Barlach down the stairs. The inspector stopped in the front door:

"There's Schmied's blue Mercedes."

Tschanz said he had bought it, on an installment plan. "Someone has to own it," he said, and got in. Barlach sat down next to him, and Tschanz drove across the Bahnhofplatz toward Bethlehem hospital. Barlach grumbled:

"You're driving via Ins again."

"I love this route."

Barlach rested his eyes on the fields that had been washed clean by the rain. Everything was steeped in a calm, bright light. The sun in the sky was mild and warm and was already sinking toward evening. Both men were silent. Only once, between Kerzers and Muntschemier, did Tschanz speak.

"Frau Schönler told me you took a folder from Schmied's room."

"Nothing official, Tschanz, just personal things."

Tschanz made no comment and asked no more questions. But Barlach had to tap his finger against the speedometer, which was showing eighty miles an hour.

"Not so fast, Tschanz, not so fast. Not that I'm scared, but my stomach can't take it. I'm an old man."

13

The writer received them in his study. It was an old, low-ceilinged room, and as the two men stepped in they were forced to stoop as if under a yoke. Outside, the little white dog with the black head was still barking, and somewhere in the house a child was crying. The writer sat in front by the gothic window, dressed in overalls and a brown leather jacket. He swiveled in his chair to face the visitors. Without rising from his desk, which was covered with papers, and after a perfunctory greeting, he demanded to know what the police wanted of him. "He's impolite," Barlach thought, "and he doesn't like policemen. Writers have never liked policemen." The old man decided to be careful. Tschanz, too, was unpleasantly affected. "He's observing us," they both thought. "If we don't watch out, we'll end up in a book." With a gesture of his hand, the writer invited them to sit down. But the moment they sank into the soft armchairs, they noted with surprise that they were seated in the light of the small window, and that the writer in his low green room filled with books was cunningly hidden from their view by the glare that fell into their eyes.

"We're looking into the case of police officer Schmied," the old man began, "who was murdered above Twann."

"I know. The case of Doctor Prantl, who was spying on Gastmann," replied the dark mass between the window and themselves.

"Gastmann told me about it." For a brief moment the writer's face was revealed as he lit a cigarette. A grin twisted his features. "You want my alibi?" Then the match went out.

"No," Barlach said.

"You don't think I could have committed the murder?" asked the writer, noticeably disappointed.

"No," Barlach replied dryly, "not you."

The writer moaned. "There we are again. Writers are sadly underestimated in Switzerland!"

The old man laughed. "If you really want to know: we already have your alibi, naturally. At twelve thirty on the night of the murder you met the bailiff and walked home together with him. The bailiff said you were in high spirits."

"I know. The policeman of Twann questioned the bailiff twice about me. And everyone who lives here. Even my mother-in-law. So you did suspect me after all," the writer noted with pride. "That's literary success of a sort!" And Barlach thought: so that's the famous vanity of writers, this craving to be taken seriously. All three men fell silent, and Tschanz tried hard to make out the writer's features. It was impossible to see him in this light.

"So what else do you want?" the writer finally hissed.

"Do you see Gastmann often?"

"What is this—an interrogation?" asked the dark mass, pushing itself more squarely in front of the window. "I don't have time for that right now."

"Come on, don't be so mean," said the inspector. "All we want is to talk a little." The writer let out a grunt, Barlach began again. "Do you see Gastmann often?"

"Now and then."

"Why?"

The old man expected another angry reply; but the writer just laughed, blew a big cloud of smoke in both their faces, and replied:

"He's an interesting character, this Gastmann, Inspector, he's the type who attracts writers like flies. And he's a wonderful cook, just amazing, let me tell you!"

And tell them he did. He told of Gastmann's culinary artistry, describing one dish after the other. For five minutes the policemen paid polite attention, and then for another five minutes; but when, after fifteen minutes, the writer was still singing the praises of Gastmann's cooking, Tschanz stood up and said he was sorry, but he and his colleague had not come to discuss food. Barlach however, whose spirits had thoroughly revived, contradicted him. "Not true," he said, "I'm extremely interested in this subject," and proceeded to rhapsodize about the culinary magic of the Turks, the Rumanians, the Bulgarians, the Yugoslavs, the Czechs, until the two men were tossing exotic recipes back and forth with the tireless enthusiasm of boys playing catch. Tschanz was sweating and cursing under his breath. The delights of the palate were quite evidently infinite and inexhaustible. But finally, after forty-five minutes, the two men stopped, exhausted, as if they had eaten long and heartily and had reached the end of their appetite. The writer lit himself a cigar. The room was silent. The child next door started crying again. The dog was barking downstairs. Then Tschanz suddenly spoke.

"Did Gastmann kill Schmied?"

The question was primitive, the old man shook his head, and the dark mass in front of them said, "You don't beat around the bush, do you?"

"I would appreciate an answer," Tschanz said firmly, leaning forward. But the writer's face remained hidden in darkness.

Barlach wondered how the man would react.

The writer remained calm.

"When was the policeman killed?" he asked.

"Before midnight," Tschanz replied.

"I don't know whether the rules of logic apply for the police," the writer said. "I rather doubt it. But since the police so cleverly found out that I met the bailiff at twelve thirty on the road to Tschernelz, it would seem that I must have taken leave of Gastmann no more than ten minutes earlier, in which case Gastmann is not very likely to have been the killer."

Tschanz wanted to know whether any other guests were present at Gastmann's at that time.

The writer answered in the negative.

"Did Schmied leave with the others?"

"Doctor Prantl was in the habit of being the penultimate guest to leave the party," the writer replied with a touch of sarcasm.

"And the last to leave?"

"That was me."

Tschanz wouldn't let go. "Were both servants present?"

"I don't know."

"How about a straight answer."

"You got a straight answer. I never pay attention to this type of servant."

With a desperation and lack of restraint that made the inspector feel acutely uncomfortable, Tschanz demanded to know whether the writer considered Gastmann a good or a bad man. "If we don't end up in his next novel," Barlach thought, "it'll be a miracle."

The writer blew such a thick cloud of smoke in Tschanz's face that the officer began to cough. Then silence descended on the room again. Even the child next door was quiet.

"Gastmann is a bad man," the writer finally said.

"And yet you keep visiting him, and for no other reason than that he's a good cook?" Tschanz asked indignantly after recovering from another coughing spell.

"For no other reason."

"I don't understand that."

The writer laughed. "I'm kind of a policeman myself," he said. "Except I have no state power, no body of laws, and no prisons to back me up. But my job is a lot like yours: I keep an eye on people."

Bewildered, Tschanz stopped asking questions, and Barlach said, "I understand." After a while, he added:

"I'm afraid that in his exaggerated zeal my subordinate Tschanz has forced us into an impasse from which I won't escape without losing a few hairs. But youthful impetuousness has its good points. Now that an unbridled ox has trampled a path for us" (Tschanz grew red with anger when the inspector said this), "let's stay with the questions and answers that have already fallen and make the best of them—take the bull by the horns, if you will. What is your opinion of this whole affair, sir? Is Gastmann capable of committing murder?"

It had become darker in the room, but it didn't occur to the writer to turn on the light. Instead he sat down in the windowsill, leaving the two policemen crouching in their armchairs like prisoners in a cave.

"I believe Gastmann is capable of every imaginable crime." The voice from the window was brutal, with a hint of sly malice in it. "But I am convinced that he is not the man who murdered Schmied."

"You know Gastmann well," Barlach said.

"I'm starting to get a picture of him," the writer said.

"*Your* picture of him," the old man coolly corrected the massive silhouette in the window sill.

"What fascinates me about him is not so much his cooking— though I must say there's hardly anything else that thrills me these days—but that here is a man who is actually—not just possibly— a nihilist," said the writer. "A slogan in the flesh. It takes your breath away."

"Listening to a writer takes your breath away too," the inspector remarked dryly.

"Maybe Gastmann has done more good than the three of us sitting here in this crooked little room," the writer continued. "When I say he's bad, it's because good and evil are, for him, just a matter of whim, and he would go to any length in either direction simply because the mood strikes him. He would never do anything evil just for the sake of gain, the way others commit crimes, for money, women, or power. But he would do it for no reason at all—maybe. Because for him, two things are always possible, good and evil, and it's chance that decides which it will be."

"You're deducing this as if it were mathematics," the old man retorted.

"It is mathematics," the writer replied. "You could construct his counterpart in evil the way you can construct a geometric figure as the mirror image of another one, and I'm sure that there is such a man—somewhere. Maybe you'll meet him too. If you meet the one, you'll meet the other."

"Sounds like a program," the old man said.

"Well, it is a program, and why not," said the writer. "My idea of Gastmann's mirror image is a man who would be a criminal because the idea of evil represents his ethics, his philosophy, to which he would be as fanatically committed as a saint might be devoted to the good."

The inspector suggested they get back to Gastmann, who was closer to his immediate interests.

"As you wish," said the writer. "Back to Gastmann, Inspector. Back to this one pole of evil. For him evil is not the expression of a philosophy or a biological drive, it is his freedom: the freedom of nothingness."

"Some freedom. I wouldn't give a cent for it," the old man replied.

"Nor should you give a cent for it," returned the other. "But one could spend a lifetime studying this man and this freedom of his."

"A lifetime," said the old man.

The writer was silent. He seemed unwilling to say anything further.

"I'm dealing with a real Gastmann," the old man finally said. "With a man who lives near Lamlingen on the Tessenberg plain and gives parties that cost a police lieutenant his life. I have to know whether the picture you have drawn for me is a picture of Gastmann or a product of your imagination."

"Our imagination," the writer said.

The inspector said nothing.

"I don't know," the writer said. He rose from his seat and stepped up to his visitors. Evidently he expected them to leave. He shook Barlach's hand, and not Tschanz's. "That's something I've never concerned myself with," he said. "I leave that to the police."

14

The two policemen walked back to their car, followed by the little white dog, which barked at them furiously, and Tschanz sat down at the wheel.

"I don't like this writer," he said. Barlach arranged his coat before he got in. The little dog had climbed onto a low stone wall and continued barking.

"Now to Gastmann's place," Tschanz said, and started the motor. The old man shook his head.

"To Bern."

They drove downhill in the direction of Ligerz, into a land that opened out far below, at a tremendous depth. All around them, the elements lay spread out far and wide: stone, earth, and water. They were driving in the shade, but the sun, which had sunk behind the Tessenberg, was still shining on the lake, the island, the hills, the foothills of the mountains, the glaciers on the horizon, and the immense towering heaps of cloud floating along in the blue oceans of the sky. The old man gazed steadily at the ceaselessly shifting, already wintry weather. It's always the same, he thought, no matter how much it changes it's always the same. But as the road suddenly swerved and the lake lay vertically beneath them like a bulging shield, Tschanz stopped the car.

"I have to talk to you, Inspector," he said in an agitated tone.

"What do you want?" Barlach asked, looking down at the huge drop by the side of the road.

"We have to see Gastmann, it's logical, it's the only lead we've got. And above all, we have to question his servants."

Barlach leaned back and sat there, gray and well groomed, scrutinizing the young man by his side through cold, narrowed eyes.

"My God, Tschanz, we can't always do the logical thing. Lutz doesn't want us to visit Gastmann. That's understandable, since he had to hand over the case to the attorney general. Let's wait for the government's ruling. It's a touchy business, we're dealing with foreigners." Barlach's casual manner drove Tschanz into a rage.

"That's nonsense!" he shouted. "Lutz is sabotaging the investigation for political reasons. Von Schwendi is his friend and Gastmann's lawyer, don't you see what's going on?"

Not a muscle moved in Barlach's face. "It's good that we're alone, Tschanz. Lutz may have acted prematurely, but his reasons were sound. The mystery lies with Schmied and not with Gastmann."

"It's our job to look for the truth!" Tschanz shouted the words into the mountainous clouds drifting overhead. "The truth and nothing but the truth! The truth about Schmied's murderer!"

"You're right," Barlach repeated, coldly and unemotionally. "The truth about Schmied's murderer."

The young policeman placed his hand on the old man's left shoulder and looked into his impenetrable face.

"And that's why we have to use every means at our disposal. And use them against Gastmann. If this is going to be a real investigation, it can't have any holes in it. You say we can't always do the logical thing. But in this case we *have* to. We can't skip Gastmann."

"Gastmann is not the killer," Barlach said dryly.

"It's possible that Gastmann ordered the killing. We have to interrogate the servants!" Tschanz retorted.

"I don't see the slightest reason why Gastmann should have wanted Schmied dead," the old man said. "We must look for the criminal where the crime would make sense, and that, I'm afraid, is the attorney general's business and not ours," he continued.

"The writer also thinks Gastmann did it," Tschanz exclaimed.

"You think so too?" Barlach asked, with a glowering look.

"Me too, Inspector."

"Then you're the only one," Barlach noted. "The writer just considers him capable of any crime under the sun, there's a difference. The writer didn't say a thing about Gastmann's actions, only about his potential."

Now Tschanz lost his patience. He gripped the old man's shoulders.

"For years I've stood in the shadow, Inspector," he gasped. "I've always been left out, ignored, treated like dirt, like some kind of glorified mailman!"

"I won't deny it, Tschanz," Barlach said, still staring fixedly into the young man's desperate eyes. "For years you stood in the shadow of the man who has now been murdered."

"Just because he went to better schools! Just because he knew Latin."

"You're not being fair to him," Barlach replied. "Schmied was the best criminologist I have ever known."

"And now," Tschanz shouted, "now that I finally have an opportunity, I'm expected to let it go down the drain, my one chance to get a promotion—all because of some stupid diplomatic maneuver! Only you can change this, Inspector, talk to Lutz, only you can get him to let me go to Gastmann."

"No, Tschanz," Barlach said, "I can't do that." His subordinate shook him, as if trying to shake sense into a naughty boy, and then he screamed:

"Talk to Lutz, talk to him!"

But the old man would not be swayed. "I can't, Tschanz," he said. "I'm not up for this sort of thing any more. I'm old and sick. I need some rest. You'll have to help yourself."

"Very well," Tschanz said, abruptly taking his hands off Barlach and putting them on the wheel again. He was quivering and deathly pale. "Then don't. You can't help me."

They drove on downhill toward Ligerz.

"You spent your vacation in Grindelwald, didn't you?" the old man asked. "Pension Eiger?"

"Yes, sir."

"Quiet and not too expensive?"

"Just as you say, sir."

"Very well, Tschanz, I'll be driving there tomorrow morning for a rest. I need the altitude. I have a week's sick leave."

Tschanz did not answer immediately. Only after they had turned into the Neuenburg-Biel highway, he said, and his voice sounded normal again:

"Altitude isn't always the best thing, Inspector."

15

That same evening Barlach went to the Bärenplatz to see his internist, Dr. Samuel Hungertobel. The streetlights were already lit, night was closing in, the darkness deepening by the minute. Barlach looked down on the old square from the doctor's window, watched the surging flood of people while Hungertobel packed up his instruments. Barlach and Hungertobel's acquaintance went back to their boyhood; they had gone to school together.

"Your heart's in good shape," Hungertobel said. "Thank God."

"Have you kept notes on my case?" Barlach asked him.

"A whole briefcase full," the doctor replied, pointing to a stack of papers on his desk. "That's all about your illness."

"You haven't told anyone about my illness, have you, Hungertobel?" Barlach asked.

"But Hans?!" said the other old man, "that's confidential, you know that!"

Down on the square, a Mercedes appeared. Its bright blue color lit up as it rolled under a light. Then it stopped among several parked cars. Barlach narrowed his eyes to see more clearly. Tschanz stepped out, followed by a young woman with a white raincoat and long blond flowing hair.

"Did anyone ever break in here, Samuel?" the inspector asked.

"Why do you ask?"

"Just wondering."

"There was a day when my desk was messed up," Hungertobel said. "And your case history was lying on top of the desk. No money had been taken, even though there was plenty inside the desk."

"And why didn't you report it?"

The doctor scratched his head. "As I said, no money had been taken. Actually I wanted to report it anyway. But then I forgot about it."

"I see," Barlach said. "You forgot. I guess burglars can count on you." And he thought: "So that's how Gastmann knows." He looked down at the square again. Tschanz was entering the Italian restaurant with the young woman. "On the day of his funeral," Barlach thought, and turned away from the window. He looked at Hungertobel, who was sitting at his desk, writing.

"So how am I doing?"

"Are you having any pains?"

The old man told him about his attack.

"That's bad news, Hans," Hungertobel said, "We'll have to operate within the next three days. There's no other way."

"I feel better than ever."

"In four days you'll have another attack, Hans," said the doctor, "and that one you won't survive."

"So I've got two days left. Two days. And on the morning of the third day, you'll perform the operation. Tuesday morning."

"Tuesday morning," Hungertobel said.

"And after that I'll have another year to live, right, Samuel?" Barlach said, fixing an impenetrable gaze on his old friend. Hungertobel jumped up and paced through the room.

"Where did you get this nonsense!"

"From the person who read my case history."

"Are you the burglar?" the doctor exclaimed in great agitation.

Barlach shook his head. "No, it wasn't me. But it's a fact nonetheless, Samuel: just one more year."

"Just one more year," Hungertobel replied, sat down on a chair

that stood against the wall of his office, and looked helplessly at Barlach, who was standing in the middle of the room, looking cold and
remote in his isolation, stolid and humble, and with such a forlorn
expression on his face that the doctor lowered his eyes.

16

Barlach woke with a start at two o'clock in the morning. At first he attributed his abrupt awakening to the effects of Hungertobel's unaccustomed prescription: he had gone to bed early and, for the first time, taken a sleeping pill. But then it seemed to him that he had been roused by some kind of noise. He was preternaturally alert and clearheaded, as often happens when we wake with a start; nevertheless it took a few moments—each one of which seemed an eternity—before he found his bearings. He was not in the room where he usually slept, but in the library; for he had anticipated a difficult night and had intended to read; but he must have suddenly fallen into a deep sleep. He passed his hands over his body. He was still dressed, and had merely covered himself with a woolen blanket. He listened. Something fell to the floor, it was the book he had been reading. The darkness in the windowless room was profound, but not complete; a weak light came in through the open door of the bedroom, the flickering glow of the stormy night. He heard the wind howling from afar. Gradually he made out the forms of a bookcase and a chair, and the edge of the table, and on top of it his revolver. Then he suddenly felt a draft, a window banged in the bedroom, and the door closed with a violent bang. Immediately afterward the old man heard a slight clicking noise in the hallway. He understood. Someone had opened the front door and had entered the hall without considering the possibility of a draft. Barlach stood up and turned on the floor lamp.

He took the revolver and released the safety catch. At that moment the intruder turned on the light in the hallway. Barlach, who could see the shining lamp through the half open door, was surprised, for he could see no meaning in this action. By the time he understood, it was too late. He saw the silhouette of an arm and a hand reaching into the lamp; then the flare of a blue light, and darkness: the stranger had torn the lamp out of the ceiling and blown the fuse. Barlach stood in complete darkness. The intruder had taken up the challenge and set the conditions: Barlach would have to fight in the dark. The old man gripped his weapon and cautiously opened the door to the bedroom. He entered the room. A vague light fell through the windows, hardly discernible at first, but stronger as the eyes became accustomed to it. Barlach leaned against the wall between the bed and the window facing the river; the other window, facing the neighbor's house, was on his right. Thus he stood in impenetrable shadow. The disadvantage of his position was that he could not retreat, but he hoped his invisibility would make up for that. The door to the library stood in the dim light of the windows. He would see the outline of the stranger's body if he came in. Now the narrow beam of a flashlight flared in the library, glided searchingly along the books, across the floor, the armchair, and finally reached the desk, revealing the snake-knife. Again Barlach saw the hand through the open door. It was sheathed in a brown leather glove. It groped along the table and grasped the handle of the snake-knife. Barlach raised the gun, aimed. The flashlight went out. Foiled, the old man lowered his weapon and waited. Looking out the window from where he stood, he sensed the black volumes of ceaselessly roiling water, the towering structures of the city on the other side of the river, the cathedral stabbing the sky like an arrow, and above it the drifting clouds. He stood immobile, waiting for the enemy who had come to kill him. His eyes bored through the vague opening of the door. He waited. Everything was quiet, lifeless. Then the clock struck in the hallway: three. He listened. Faintly he heard the distant ticking of the clock. Somewhere a car honked, then it drove by. People leaving a bar. Once he thought he heard breathing, but he must have been mistaken. And so he stood there, and somewhere in his house was the other man, and engulfing them both, the black cloak of night, with the snake concealed beneath it, the dagger in search of his heart. The old man scarcely breathed. He stood clutching his gun, scarcely aware of the cold sweat running down his neck. He thought of nothing—not of Gastmann, not of Lutz, nor of the sickness gnawing at his body hour after hour and about to destroy the life he was now defending for no other reason than that he desperately wanted to live, and only to live. His whole being was reduced to a single eye searching the night, a single ear testing the minutest sound, a single hand firmly locked around the cool metal of the gun. When the murderer's presence betrayed itself to him, it wasn't as he had expected; he sensed a vague coldness touching his cheek, a slight change in the air. For a long time he could not explain it to himself, until he guessed that the door leading from the bedroom to the dining room had opened. The stranger had outwitted the old man again, he had penetrated the bedroom by a roundabout route, invisible, inaudible, inexorable, with the snake-knife in his hand. Barlach knew now that he had to be the first to act. Old and mortally sick as he was, he would have to begin the battle, the fight for a life that might last one more year, provided that Hungertobel applied his knife wisely and accurately. Barlach aimed his revolver at the window facing the Aare River. Then he fired, and again, three times in rapid succession through the splintering glass out into the river, and lowered himself to the floor. He heard a hissing sound above him. It was the knife that now stuck in the wall, quivering. But already the old man had achieved what he wanted: light appeared in the other window, it came from the house next door, the neighbors were leaning out of their opened windows; bewildered and terrified, they were staring into the night. Barlach rose to his feet. The neighbors' lights lit up the bedroom. A shadowy form slipped away from the dining room door. Then the front door slammed shut, and after that, pulled by the draft, the door to the library slammed, and following that the dining room door, one crash after the other, and finally the window knocked against its frame. The people next door were still staring into the night. The old man by the wall did not move. He stood there, immobile, still holding the weapon, as if he had lost all consciousness of time. The neighbors withdrew, and turned off their lights. Bärlach stood by the wall, steeped in darkness again, at one with it, alone in the house.

17

Half an hour passed before he went to the hallway and looked for his flashlight. He called up Tschanz and asked him to come. Then he replaced the blown fuse, and the lights went on again. Barlach sat down in his armchair and listened into the night. A car drove up in the front of the house, braked sharply. Again the front door opened, again he heard a step. Tschanz came into the room.

"Someone tried to kill me," the inspector said. Tschanz was pale. He was hatless, his hair was disheveled, his pajama pants showed at the bottom of his winter coat. Together they went into the bedroom. With an effort, Tschanz pulled the knife out of the wall. It was deeply embedded in the wood.

"With this?"

"With that, Tschanz."

The young policeman examined the shattered windowpane.

"You shot through the window, Inspector?" he asked, surprised.

Barlach told him everything. "That was the best thing you could do," Tschanz murmured.

They went into the hallway, and Tschanz picked up the lamp from the floor.

"Clever," he said, not without admiration, and put it aside. Then they went back to the library. The old man stretched out on the couch, covered himself with the blanket, and lay there, helpless, feeling suddenly terribly old, almost shriveled. Tschanz was still holding the snake knife in his hand.

"Didn't you get a glimpse of him?" he asked.

"No. He was careful and withdrew quickly. All I saw for a moment was a brown leather glove."

"That's not much."

"It's nothing. But even though I didn't see him, even though I could hardly hear him breathe, I know who it was. I know it; I know it."

The old man said all this almost inaudibly. Tschanz weighed the knife in his hand, looking down at the gray, prostrate figure before him, this tired old man, these hands that lay next to the frail old body like withered flowers next to a corpse. Then he saw Barlach's gaze. It was focused on him, calm, clear, and inscrutable. Tschanz laid the knife on the desk.

"You must go to Grindelwald this morning, you're sick. Or would you rather not go? It might not be the right thing, the altitude. It's really winter up there."

"No, no, I'm going."

"Then you should get some sleep. Do you want me to stay here and keep watch?"

"No, Tschanz, you can go," the inspector said.

"Good night," Tschanz said and slowly walked out. The old man said nothing, he seemed to have fallen asleep. Tschanz opened the front door, stepped out, closed the door. Slowly he walked the few steps to the street, closed the garden door, which had stood open. Then he turned toward the house again. It was still pitch dark. All things seemed lost in the night, even the houses next door. A single street light burned far above, a lost star in the gloom of a night filled with sorrow, filled with the dark steady surge of the river. Tschanz stood there, and suddenly he cursed softly under his breath. He kicked open the garden gate and strode resolutely up the path to the front door, the same way he had come. He grasped the door handle and pushed it down. But now the door was locked.

Barlach got up at six without having slept. It was Sunday. The old man washed, changed his clothes. Then he called for a taxi, intending to eat in the dining car. He put on his warm winter coat and left the house, stepping out into the cold winter morning, but without a valise. The sky was clear. A drunken student staggered by, stinking of beer, and greeted him. "Poor Blaser," Barlach thought. "He just failed his exam for the second time. No wonder he's drinking." The taxi drove up, stopped. It was one of those large American cars. The driver had turned up his collar, Barlach could hardly see his eyes. The driver opened the door for him.

"To the station," Barlach said, getting in. The car started.

"Well," said a voice next to him, "how are you? Did you sleep well?"

Barlach turned his head. In the other corner sat Gastmann. He was wearing a gray raincoat and his arms were folded. He was wearing brown leather gloves. The way he sat there, he looked like a mocking old peasant. The driver in front turned his head and looked back at Barlach, grinning. He was one of the servants. Barlach realized he had stepped into a trap.

"What do you want from me now?" he asked.

"You're still after me. You talked to that writer," said the one in the corner, and his voice sounded threatening.

"It's my job."

The other kept his eyes on him. "There isn't a single one who took up my case, Barlach, who's still alive."

The man in front drove up the Aargauerstalden at a furious speed.

"I'm still alive. And I've always been on your case," the inspector said calmly.

They were both silent.

Still racing, the driver headed for Viktoriaplatz. An old man limping across the street got out of the way in the nick of time.

"Why don't you watch what you're doing!" Barlach said angrily.

"Drive faster," Gastmann said with a cutting voice. His eyes looked mocking as he scrutinized the old man. "I love the speed of machines."

The inspector shuddered. He did not like being enclosed in an airless space. They flew across the bridge, passing a streetcar, over the silver ribbon of water far below them into the welcoming streets of the city, which were still vacant and deserted, under a glassy sky.

"I would advise you to give up," Barlach said, stuffing his pipe. "You've lost the game, it's time to concede."

The old man looked at the dark arcades gliding past them, and he noticed the shadowy figures of two policemen in front of Lang's book store.

"Geissbühler and Zumsteg," he thought, and then: "I really should pay for that Fontane novel."

"Our game," he finally replied, "— we can't give it up. You became guilty on that night in Turkey because you proposed a bet, Gastmann, and I became guilty because I accepted it."

They drove past the House of Parliament.

"You still think I killed Schmied?" Gastmann asked.

"I didn't believe that for a moment," the old man replied. He watched indifferently as the other man lit his pipe, and continued:

"I haven't succeeded in proving your guilt of the crimes you've committed. So this time I'll prove you guilty of something you didn't do."

Gastmann scrutinized the inspector's face.

"I never thought of this possibility," he said. "I'll have to be careful."

The inspector said nothing.

"You may be more dangerous than I realized, old man," Gastmann said pensively from his corner.

The car stopped. They had reached the train station.

"This is the last time I'll be talking to you, Barlach," Gastmann said. "The next time I'll kill you. Assuming you survive your operation."

"You're wrong," Barlach said, looking old as he stood shivering on the square in the early morning light. "You won't kill me. I am the only one who knows you, so I'm the only one who can judge you. I have judged you, Gastmann, I have sentenced you to death. You will not survive this day. The executioner I have chosen will come to you today. He will kill you, because, by God, this is something that simply has to be done."

Gastmann flinched and stared at the old man in astonishment. But Barlach walked into the station with his hands buried in his coat pockets. Without turning around, he walked into the dark building, which was gradually filling up with people.

"You fool!" Gastmann suddenly shouted after the inspector, so loudly that several passersby turned around. "Fool!" But Barlach was no longer visible.

18

The gradually, steadily rising day was clear and powerful. The sun, a perfect ball, cast hard and long shadows, which became shorter the higher it rolled. The city lay there, a white shell, sucking up the light, swallowing it into her narrow streets in order to spew it out after nightfall as thousands of lights, a monster perpetually busy with spawning and poisoning and burying an ever-growing quantity of new human beings. The radiance of the morning grew by the minute, a shining shield above the diminishing echoes of the church bells. Tschanz waited for an hour, looking pale in the light that was reflected from the walls. Restlessly he walked to and fro beneath the arcades in front of the cathedral, looking up at the gargoyles from time to time, demons that stared at the sunlit pavement with savage, contorted expressions. Finally the portals opened, releasing a vast stream of people who had come to hear Luthi, the famous preacher, in person, but Tschanz immediately saw her white raincoat. Anna walked up to him. She said she was glad to see him and gave him her hand. They walked up the Kesslergasse, surrounded by a swarm of churchgoers, old and young: here a professor, there a baker's wife in her Sunday finery, two students with a girl, several dozen officials, teachers, all of them clean, all of them washed, all of them hungry, all of them looking forward to a sumptuous Sunday meal. They reached the Kasinoplatz, crossed it, and went down into the Marzili. They stopped on the bridge.

"Fräulein Anna," Tschanz said, "today I'm going to catch Ulrich's murderer."

"Do you know who he is?" she asked, surprised.

He looked at her. She stood before him, pale and slim. "I believe I do," he said. "Once I've caught him, will you be . . ." He hesitated. "Will you be for me what you were for your deceased fiancé?"

Anna did not answer immediately. She pulled her coat more tightly around her as if she were cold. A slight breeze disturbed her blond hair. Then she said:

"We've agreed on that."

They shook hands, and Anna walked on to the other shore. He looked after her. Her white coat gleamed among the birch trees, disappeared among other pedestrians, reemerged, and finally vanished. Then he went to the train station, where he had left his car. He drove to Ligerz. It was almost noon when he got there, for he drove slowly, stopping occasionally to walk in the fields and smoke before returning to the car and driving on. In Ligerz he parked in front of the station. Then he climbed the steps leading up to the church. He was calm now. The lake was deep blue, the vines had lost their leaves, and the earth between them was brown and loose. But Tschanz saw none of these things. He climbed at a steady and regular pace, without turning back and without pausing. The path led steeply uphill, framed by white walls, past vineyard after vineyard. Tschanz kept climbing, calmly, slowly, steadily, his right hand in the pocket of his coat. From time to time lizards crossed his path. Buzzards rose into the sky, the land trembled under the blazing sun as if it were summer. He climbed on and on, relentlessly, unremittingly. Later he left the vineyards and slipped into the forest. It was cooler there. The Jura cliffs shone stark and white between the tree trunks. He climbed higher and higher, always at the same pace, until he reached the fields. This was farming and pasture land; the path rose more gently. He walked past a cemetery, a rectangle bordered by a gray wall, with a wide-open gate. Black-clad women walked on the paths, a bent old man stood watching the stranger as he marched past with his right hand in his coat pocket.

He reached Prèles, walked past the Bear Inn and directed his steps toward Lamboing. The air over the high plateau was motionless and clear. All things, even those in the far distance, stood out with extreme clarity. Only the ridge of the Chasseral was covered with snow, everything else was a brilliant light brown interspersed here and there with white walls and red roofs and black bands of farmland.

Steadily, Tschanz walked on; the sun was shining on his back, casting his shadow ahead of him. The road dipped, he was approaching the sawmill, now the sun was at his side. He marched without thinking, without seeing, impelled by *one* purpose, possessed by *one* passion. A dog barked somewhere, came up to him, sniffed at his feet, and ran away. Tschanz walked on, always on the right-hand side of the street, always at the same pace, toward the house that was now rising up from the brown landscape, framed by bare poplars. Tschanz left the road and walked through the fields. His shoes sank into the warm earth of an unploughed field; he walked on. Then he reached the gate. It was open, Tschanz went through it. In the courtyard stood an American car. Tschanz payed it no attention. He went to the front door. It, too, was open. Tschanz stepped into an entrance hall, opened a second door, and walked into a hall that comprised the whole ground floor. Tschanz stopped. Glaring light fell through the windows facing him. In front of him, not five paces away, stood Gastmann. Next to him his gigantic servants, immobile and menacing, two butchers. All three were wearing coats. Towering heaps of valises stood by their sides. They were about to leave.

Tschanz stood still.

"So it's you," Gastmann said, looking with slight surprise at the calm, pale face of the policeman and at the open door behind him.

Then he started to laugh. "So that's what the old man meant! Not bad, not bad at all!"

Gastmann's eyes were wide open, and Tschanz saw them light up with a flash of ghostly mirth.

Calmly, without saying a word, almost slowly, one of the butchers pulled a pistol out of his pocket and fired. Tschanz felt a blow against his left shoulder, pulled his right hand out of his pocket and threw himself to the side. Then he fired three shots point blank into Gastmann's laughter, which died away slowly as if in an infinite void.

19

Informed by a telephone call from Tschanz, Charnel sped over from Lamboing, Clenin rushed in from Twann, and the crime squad from Biel. Tschanz was found bleeding near the three corpses. A second shot had hit him in the left forearm. The gun battle must have been brief, but each of the three dead men had found time to fire. A gun was found on each of them. One of the servants was still holding his weapon in a tight grip. Tschanz was unable to follow what happened after Charnel's arrival. He fainted twice while the doctor from Neuveville bandaged his wounds; however, his injuries turned out to be harmless. Some villagers came later, peasants, workers, women. The courtyard was so crowded that the police had to bar the entrance. One young woman managed to push her way into the hall and threw herself screaming onto Gastmann's body. It was the waitress, Charnel's fiancée. He stood by, red with anger. Then Tschanz was carried to the car through the throng of retreating peasants.

"There they are, all three of them," Lutz said the next morning, with a gesture indicating the corpses, but his voice did not sound triumphant; it sounded sad and tired.

Von Schwendi nodded, dismayed. The colonel had driven to Biel with Lutz on his client's instructions. They had come into the room where the bodies lay. A slanting shaft of light fell through a small barred window. The two men stood there in their coats and felt cold. Lutz had red eyes. He had spent the whole night reading Gastmann's journals, which were written in shorthand and difficult to decipher.

Lutz buried his hands deeper in his pockets. "That's how we are, von Schwendi," he began again, almost softly. "We're so scared of each other that we set up armed camps called states. We surround ourselves with guards of all sorts, with policemen, with soldiers, with public opinion; what good does it do?" Lutz twisted his face into a grimace, his eyes bulged, and he laughed. It came out as a hollow, goatish bleat in the cold, barren room. "A single dunce at the head of a world power, Councillor, and we'll be carried off by the floods. One Gastmann, and already our cordons are cut through, our outposts outflanked."

Von Schwendi realized it would be best to bring the examining magistrate back down to earth, but he didn't quite know how. "Exactly," he finally said. "Our circles are shamelessly exploited by all sorts of people. It's embarrassing, highly embarrassing."

"No one had any idea," Lutz said reassuringly.

"And Schmied?" asked the national councillor, glad to have found the key word.

"We found a folder in Gastmann's possession that had belonged to Schmied. It contained information about Gastmann's life and conjectures about his crimes. Schmied was trying to apprehend Gastmann. He did this on his own private recognizance. An error for which he had to pay with his life; for we have proof that Schmied's murder was ordered by Gastmann: Schmied had to have been killed with the same weapon one of the servants was holding when Tschanz shot him. The examination of the weapon confirmed this immediately. The motive for the murder is also clear: Gastmann was afraid of being exposed by Schmied. Schmied should have confided in us. But he was young and ambitious."

Barlach came into the morgue. When Lutz saw the old man, he became melancholy and buried his hands in his pockets. "Well, Inspector," he said, shifting his weight from one foot to the other, "it's nice that we're meeting here. You have come back in time from your vacation, and I, too, have rushed over here with my state councillor and arrived in good time, as you see. There are the dead, served up for our delectation. We have had our quarrels, Barlach, many times. I was in favor of a super-sophisticated police force with all the latest paraphernalia, including the atom bomb if I could have had my way, and you, Inspector, wanted something more human, a sort of rural gendarmerie stocked with good-natured grandfathers. Let's bury the hatchet. We were both wrong. Tschanz refuted us by the very unscientific but straightforward use of his revolver. I don't want to know the details. Very well, it was self-defense, we have to believe him, and why shouldn't we. The catch was worth it, the men he shot deserved a thousand deaths, as they say, and if scientific method had prevailed, we would now be poking around in foreign affairs. I will have to promote Tschanz; while you and I, I'm afraid, are left looking like fools. The Schmied case is closed."

Lutz lowered his head, bewildered by the old man's enigmatic silence, and felt his proud posture collapsing into that of a proper, conscientious official. He cleared his throat and, noticing von Schwendi's embarrassment, blushed. Slowly, then, accompanied by the colonel, he walked out of the room and into the darkness of the hallway, leaving Barlach alone. The bodies lay on stretchers and were covered with black cloths. The plaster was peeling off the bare, gray walls. Barlach went to the middle stretcher and uncovered the body. It was Gastmann. Barlach bent over him slightly, holding the black cloth in his left hand. Silently he gazed into the waxen face of the dead man. There was still an amused expression on his lips. But his eyes were set even more deeply than in life, and there was no longer anything terrible lurking in those depths. Thus they met for the last time, the hunter and his prey, who now lay dead at his feet. Barlach sensed that both their lives were at an end now, and once again he looked back on the labyrinthine paths of their mysteriously intertwined lives. Now there remained nothing between them but the immensity of death, a judge whose verdict is silence. Barlach still stood slightly bent, and the pale light of the cell flickered and played equally on Barlach's face and hands and Gastmann's body, meant for both, created for both, reconciling them both. The silence of death sank down upon him, crept into him, but it gave him no peace as it had to the other man. The dead are always right. Slowly Barlach covered Gastmann's face with the cloth. This was the last time he would see him; from now on his enemy belonged to the grave. A single thought had obsessed him for years: to destroy the man who now lay at his feet in the cool gray room, covered with falling plaster as if with fine flakes of snow; and now there was nothing left for the old man but to wearily cover his enemy's face, and humbly beg for forgetfulness, the only mercy that can soothe a heart consumed by a raging fire.

20

That same evening, at eight o'clock sharp, Tschanz arrived at the old man's house in the Altenberg district. Barlach had urgently asked him to come at that hour. To his surprise, a young maid in a white apron opened the door, and as he stepped into the hallway, he heard the sounds of boiling water and roasting fat and the clatter of dishes. The maid removed the coat from his shoulders. His left arm was in a sling, but he had been able to come in his own car. The maid opened the door to the dining room, and Tschanz stopped in his tracks: the table was festively set for two people. Candles were burning in a candelabrum, and Barlach was sitting in an armchair at one end of the table, softly lit by the reddish light of the flames, the very image of imperturbable calm.

"Sit down, Tschanz," the old man called out to his guest, pointing at a second armchair that had been pulled up to the table. Tschanz sat down, stunned.

"I didn't know I was coming to dinner," he finally said.

"We have to celebrate your victory," the old man quietly replied, pushing the candelabrum a little to the side so that they could look each other fully in the face. Then he clapped his hands. The door opened, and a stately, rotund woman brought in a tray overflowing with sardines, lobster, a salad of cucumbers, tomatoes, and peas garnished with mountains of mayonnaise and eggs, and dishes with cold chicken, slices of cold roast, and salmon. Barlach helped himself to everything. Tschanz watched the man with the ailing stomach assemble a portion fit for a giant, and was so baffled he merely asked for a little potato salad.

"What shall we drink?" Barlach asked. "Ligerzer?"

"Ligerzer's fine with me," Tschanz replied as if dreaming. The maid came and filled their glasses. Barlach started to eat, helped himself to some bread, devoured the salmon, the sardines, the flesh of the red lobsters, the chicken, the salads, the mayonnaise, and the cold roast, clapped his hands, and asked for a second serving. Tschanz, who was still picking at his potato salad, looked petrified. Barlach called for a third glass of white wine.

"Let's have the pâtés and the red Neuenberger," he called out. The plates were changed. Barlach requested three pâtés, filled with goose liver, pork, and truffles.

"But you're sick, Inspector," Tschanz finally said, hesitantly.

"Not today, Tschanz, not today. This is a day for celebration. I've finally nailed Schmied's killer!"

He drained his second glass of red wine and started on his third pâté, eating without pause, stuffing himself with the world's good food, crushing each mouthful between his jaws like a demon attempting to still an unappeasable hunger. His body cast a shadow on the wall, twice his size, and the powerful movements of his arms and lowered head resembled the triumphal dance of an African chieftain. Appalled, Tschanz watched the terminally sick man's ghastly performance. He sat without moving, and was no longer eating or so much as touching his food. Nor did he once raise his glass to his lips. Barlach ordered veal cutlets, rice, French fries, green salad, and champagne. Tschanz was trembling.

"You're pretending," he said, with a choked voice. "You aren't sick at all!"

Barlach didn't answer immediately. At first he laughed, then he occupied himself with the salad, savoring each leaf, one by one. Tschanz did not dare ask the gruesome old man his question again.

"Yes, Tschanz," Barlach finally said, and his eyes flashed wildly,

"I've been pretending. I was never sick." And he shoved a piece of veal into his mouth and continued eating, incessantly, insatiably.

And now Tschanz realized that he had walked into a cunningly prepared trap, and that the door was just now falling shut behind him. Cold sweat burst from his pores. Horror gripped him like a pair of mighty arms. His realization came too late, there was no way out.

"You know, Inspector," he said softly.

"Yes, Tschanz, I know," Barlach said calmly and firmly, without raising his voice, as though commenting on a matter of indifference. "You are Schmied's murderer." Then he reached for his glass of champagne and emptied it in one draught.

"I always had the feeling that you knew," Tschanz said almost inaudibly.

The old man's face remained expressionless. Nothing seemed to interest him more than this meal; relentlessly, he heaped a second mound of rice on his plate, poured gravy over it, topped it with a veal cutlet. Once again Tschanz tried to find an escape, a defense against this fiendish eater.

"The bullet came from the gun they found on the servant," he stated defiantly. But his voice sounded disheartened.

Barlach's narrowed eyes glittered with contempt. "Nonsense, Tschanz. You know perfectly well that that was *your* gun, and that you put it in the dead man's hand. Your only cover was the fact that Gastmann was found to be a criminal."

"You'll *never* be able to prove this," Tschanz desperately exclaimed.

The old man stretched in his seat, no longer sick and decrepit but powerful and relaxed, exuding a superiority that seemed almost godlike, a tiger playing with his victim. He drank the rest of his champagne. Then he stopped the waitress, who had been walking in and out, clearing the table and bringing more food, and asked her to bring some cheese, to which he added radishes, pearl onions, and pickled cucumbers. He consumed one delicacy after another, as if to taste one last time the good things of this earth.

"Do you really not realize, Tschanz," he finally said, "that you gave me the proof of your guilt long ago? The gun was yours. You see, Gastmann's dog, which you shot in order to save me, had a bullet in his body that had to come from the same weapon that killed Schmied: *your* weapon. You yourself supplied me with the evidence I needed. You gave yourself away when you saved my life."

"When I saved your life! So that's why I couldn't find the dog when I went back," Tschanz replied mechanically. "Did you know that Gastmann had a bloodhound?"

"Yes. I had a blanket wrapped around my left arm."

"So that, too, was a trap," the murderer said with a toneless voice.

"That too. But the first proof you gave me was on Friday, when you insisted on driving to Ligerz via Ins so you could put on that farce about the 'blue Charon.' On Wednesday, Schmied drove through Zollikofen, not Ins. I knew this, because on that night, he stopped at the garage in Lyss."

"How could you know that?" Tschanz asked.

"I simply made a call. The man who drove through Ins and Erlach on that night was the murderer: you, Tschanz. You came from Grindelwald. The Pension Eiger also has a blue Mercedes. For weeks you had observed Schmied, watched his every step, jealous of his abilities, his success, his education, his girl. You knew he was investigating Gastmann, you even knew on what days he visited him, but you didn't know why. Then, by coincidence, the briefcase with the documents on his desk fell into your hands. You made a decision: to kill Schmied and take over the Gastmann case, so that you could for once enjoy some real success. It would be easy, you thought, to pin a murder on Gastmann, and you were right. So when I saw a blue Mercedes in Grindelwald, everything fell into place. You rented that car on Wednesday evening. I know you did, because I asked. The rest is simple: you drove to Schernelz through Ligerz and left the car standing in the woods near Twann. You crossed the forest by taking a short cut through the ravine, which took you to the Twann-Lamboing highway. You waited for Schmied by the cliffs, he recognized you, and stopped, surprised to see you there. He opened the door, and then you killed him. You told me so yourself.

And now you have what you wanted: his success, his position, his car, and his girlfriend."

Tschanz listened to the merciless chess player who had checkmated him and was now finishing his horrible meal. The candles were wavering, their light flickered on the faces of the two men, the shadows were growing more dense. A deadly silence reigned in this nocturnal hell. The maids were no longer coming into the room. The old man sat motionless now, scarcely breathing, his face bathed in wave after wave of flickering light, a red fire that broke against the ice of his brow and his soul.

"You played with me," Tschanz said slowly.

"I played with you," Barlach replied with a terrible gravity. "I couldn't do otherwise. You took Schmied. I had to take you."

"In order to kill Gastmann," interjected Tschanz, suddenly realizing the whole truth.

"That's it. I gave up half my life to get Gastmann convicted, and Schmied was my last hope. I put him on the tracks of the devil incarnate, like setting a noble animal on the trail of some vicious beast. But then you came along, Tschanz, with your ridiculous, criminal ambition, and destroyed my only chance. So I took *you*, you, the killer, and turned you into my most terrible weapon. Because you were driven by desperation. The killer had to find another killer. I made my goal your goal."

"It was pure hell for me," Tschanz said.

"It was hell for both of us," the old man continued with terrible calmness. "Von Schwendi's interference pushed you over the edge, you had to somehow establish that Gastmann was the murderer, because every deviation from Gastmann's trail could lead to yours. Schmied's briefcase was the only thing that could help you. You knew it was in my possession, but you didn't know that Gastmann had taken it away. That's why you attacked me on Saturday night. Also, you didn't want me to go to Grindelwald."

"You knew it was I who attacked you?" Tschanz asked with a blank, toneless voice.

"I knew that from the very first moment. Everything I did was done with the intention of driving you to the utmost desperation.

And when your despair reached the breaking point, you went to Lamboing to force a decision one way or another."

"One of Gastmann's servants fired the first shot," Tschanz said.

"I told Gastmann on Sunday morning that I was sending someone to kill him."

Tschanz reeled and felt himself turn cold as ice. "Then you pitted us both on each other, like animals!"

"Beast against beast," came the pitiless voice from the other chair.

"So you were the judge, and I was the hangman," Tschanz said, almost choking.

"That is correct," replied the old man.

"And I, who was only carrying out your will, whether I wanted to or not, I'm a criminal now, a man to be hunted!"

Tschanz stood up, leaning on the table with his uninjured right hand. Only one candle was still lit. With burning eyes Tschanz tried to make out the shape of the old man in the darkness, but all he could see was an unreal, black shadow. He made an uncertain, groping movement in the direction of his breast pocket.

"Don't do that," he heard the old man say. "It makes no sense. Lutz knows you are here with me, and the women are still in the house."

"You're right, it makes no sense," Tschanz replied softly.

"The Schmied case is settled," the old man said through the darkness of the room. "I won't betray you. But leave! Go anywhere! I don't want to see you ever again. It's enough that I judged *one* man. Go! Go!"

Tschanz lowered his head and walked out slowly, letting the door fall into the lock, and as he drove off, blending with the night, the candle went out, sputtering, and with a last sudden flare lit up the face of the old man, who had closed his eyes.

21

Barlach sat through the night in his armchair, without standing up once. The enormous, avid vitality that had flared up in him was collapsing and threatened to die altogether. The old man had taken one last, wildly audacious risk, but he had lied to Tschanz in one respect. When, at the break of dawn, Lutz came storming into his room to report with great consternation that Tschanz had been found dead in his car after being hit by a train between Twann and Ligerz, he found the inspector mortally ill. With an effort, the old man ordered him to remind Hungertobel that it was Tuesday, and that he was ready for the operation.

"Just one more year," Lutz heard the old man say as he stared through the window into the glassy morning. "Just one more year."

SUSPICION

Part One

THE SUSPICION

Inspector Barlach had checked into the Salem—the hospital over-looking the town hall and the old parts of Bern—in the beginning of November, 1948. A heart attack had delayed the urgent and difficult surgical intervention by two weeks. The operation was finally performed with success, but the surgeon's findings confirmed his belief that Barlach's sickness was incurable.

The inspector's boss, Investigating Magistrate Dr. Lutz, had twice given him up for dead and twice regained hope before an improvement finally set in shortly before Christmas. The old man slept through the holidays, but on the twenty-seventh, a Monday, he was awake and chipper, looking at old issues of *Life* magazine from the year 1945.

"They were beasts, Samuel," he said when Dr. Hungertobel stepped into his room for his regular evening visit. "Beasts." And he handed him the magazine. "You're a doctor, you can imagine this. Look at this picture from the Stutthof concentration camp! There's the camp doctor, Nehle, photographed while performing an abdominal operation on a prisoner without anesthesia."

"The Nazis did that sometimes," the doctor said, looking at the picture. But he turned pale just as he was about to put the magazine aside.

"What's the matter?" the sick man asked, surprised.

Hungertobel did not answer immediately. He put the open magazine on Barlach's bed, reached for the right upper pocket of his white smock, and pulled out a pair of horn-rimmed glasses. As he put them on, the inspector noticed the doctor's hands were trembling slightly. Then Hungertobel looked at the picture a second time.

"Why is he so nervous?" Barlach wondered.

"Nonsense," Hungertobel finally said with irritation, and put the magazine on the table with the others. "Come, give me your hand. Let's check your pulse."

There was silence for a minute. Then the doctor let go of his friend's arm and looked at the chart over the bed.

"Things are looking up, Hans."

"One more year?" Barlach asked.

Hungertobel was embarrassed. "Let's not talk about that now," he said. "You have to be careful and come back for a checkup."

"I'm always careful," the old man grumbled.

"So much the better," said Hungertobel, taking his leave.

"Hand me that issue of *Life,* will you?" the sick man said, casually, it seemed. Hungertobel gave him a magazine from the pile on the night table.

"Not that one," said the inspector, giving the doctor a slightly mocking look. "I want the one you took away from me. I can't skip over a concentration camp that easily."

Hungertobel hesitated for a moment, blushed when he saw Barlach's probing gaze, and gave him the magazine. Then he quickly walked out, as if to avoid something disagreeable. The nurse came in. The inspector asked her to take out the other magazines.

"Not that one?" the nurse asked, pointing at the magazine on Barlach's feather blanket.

"No, not that one," the old man said.

After the nurse had left, he looked at the picture again. The doctor carrying out his fiendish experiment looked calm and composed, like a stone idol. Most of his face was hidden behind a surgical mask.

The inspector carefully put the magazine in the drawer of his night table and folded his hands behind his head. His eyes were wide open, and he watched the night gradually filling the room. He did not turn on the light.

Later the nurse came and brought him his supper. It was dietary fare, and a small portion at that: oatmeal gruel. He didn't touch the lime blossom tea, which he disliked. After finishing his gruel, he turned out the light and gazed again into the darkness, the deepening, thickening shadows.

He loved to watch the lights of the city shining in through the window.

When the nurse returned to prepare the inspector for the night, he was already asleep.

At ten in the morning, Hungertobel came.

Barlach was lying with his hands behind his head, and on top of his blanket lay the open magazine. His eyes were intently focused on the doctor. Hungertobel saw that the picture in front of the old man was the one showing the concentration camp doctor.

"Won't you tell me why you turned deathly pale when I showed you this picture in *Life* magazine?" the sick man asked.

Hungertobel went to the bed, took down the chart, studied it more carefully than usual, and hung it back. "It was a silly mistake, Hans," he said. "Not worth talking about."

"Do you know this Doctor Nehle?" Barlach's voice sounded strangely agitated.

"No," Hungertobel replied. "I don't know him. He just reminded me of someone."

"The resemblance must be a strong one," the inspector said.

"It is," the doctor admitted, and looked at the picture again. Again he was visibly alarmed. "But the photograph only shows half the face," he objected. "All surgeons look alike when they're operating."

"And who does this beast remind you of?" Barlach asked relentlessly.

"But this is pointless!" Hungertobel replied. "I told you, it has to be a mistake."

"And yet you could swear it was him. Isn't that right, Samuel?"

"Well, yes," the doctor replied. "I could swear it if I didn't know that this man can't possibly be suspected of this. So let's just drop this unpleasant subject. It's not a good idea anyway, leafing through this magazine right after an operation where your own life was in jeopardy."

Then he stared at the picture again, as if hypnotized.

"That doctor there," he continued after a while, "can't possibly be the man I know, because he was in Chile during the war. So obviously it's all nonsense."

"In Chile, in Chile," Barlach said. "When did he come back, this man whom you know and who can't possibly be Nehle?"

"In forty-five."

"In Chile, in Chile," Barlach said again. "And you don't want to tell me who this picture reminds you of?"

The old doctor hesitated. He was obviously flustered.

"If I tell you the name, Hans," he finally said, "you'll end up suspecting the man."

"I'm already suspecting him," the inspector replied.

Hungertobel sighed. "You see, Hans," he said, "that's what I was afraid of. I don't want you to do that, do you understand? I am an old doctor and I don't want to feel that I've harmed someone. Your suspicion is pure insanity. You can't just suspect a person because of some photograph, and this one doesn't even show much of the face. And besides, he was in Chile, and that's a fact."

"What did he do there?" the inspector interjected.

"He directed a clinic in Santiago."

"In Chile, in Chile," Barlach said again. "That's a dangerous refrain, and not easy to check. You're right, Samuel, suspicion is a terrible thing, it comes from the devil. There's nothing like suspicion to bring out the worst in people. I know that very well, and I've often cursed my profession for it. People should stay away from suspicion. But now we've got it, and you gave it to me. I'd gladly give it back to you, old friend, if you would just forget about it yourself; because it's you who can't drop this suspicion of ours."

Hungertobel sat down by the side of the old man's bed. Helplessly he looked at the inspector. Slanting bars of sunlight fell through the curtains into the room. It was one of those beautiful days of which there were so many during that mild winter.

"I can't," the doctor finally said into the silence of the sickroom. "I can't. God help me, I can't shake off this suspicion. I know him too well. I studied with him, and twice he substituted for me. That's him in this picture. The scar above the temple from an operation, there it is. I know it, I operated on Emmenberger myself."

Hungertobel took off his glasses and put them in his right upper pocket. Then he wiped the sweat off his forehead.

"Emmenberger?" the inspector asked calmly after a while. "That's his name?"

"Now I've said it," Hungertobel answered uneasily. "Fritz Emmenberger."

"A doctor?"

"A doctor."

"And he lives in Switzerland?"

"He owns the Sonnenstein clinic on the Zürichberg," the doctor replied. "In thirty-two he emigrated to Germany and then to Chile. In forty-five he returned and took over the clinic. One of the most expensive private hospitals in Switzerland," he added in a low voice.

"Only for the rich?"

"Only for the very rich."

"Is his scientific research any good, Samuel?"

Hungertobel hesitated. "That's a hard question to answer," he said. "There was a time when he was a good researcher, but we don't really know whether he remained one. He works with methods that seem questionable to us. We hardly know anything about the hormones he's specialized in. Wherever science sets out to conquer some field, it's a free-for-all, everyone tries to rush in ahead of the fray— scientists and quacks, often combined in one person. What can you do, Hans? Emmenberger's patients love and believe in him, he is their god. That's the most important thing, I believe, for patients who are that rich and want their sickness to be another luxury; faith moves mountains, and it definitely moves hormones. So he has his successes, he is revered, and he makes money. We call him the 'heir apparent.'"

Hungertobel suddenly stopped talking, as if he regretted having revealed Emmenberger's nickname.

"The heir apparent. What's that name about?" Barlach asked.

"A lot of patients have willed their estate to the clinic," Hungertobel replied with obvious embarrassment. "It's sort of a fashion there."

"So you doctors noticed this!" the inspector said.

They both fell silent, and in that silence there was something unspoken that filled Hungertobel with fear.

"You mustn't think what you're thinking," he suddenly said, horrified.

"I'm just thinking your thoughts," the inspector calmly replied. "Let's be exact. Even if it's a crime to think what we're thinking, let's not be afraid of our thoughts. How can we overcome them—presuming they're wrong—unless we examine them, and how can we do that unless we admit them to our conscience? So what *are* we thinking, Samuel? We are thinking that Emmenberger uses methods that he learned in the concentration camp at Stutthof to force his patients to leave him their fortunes, and that then he kills them."

"No!" Hungertobel cried with feverish eyes. "No!" He stared at Barlach anxiously. "We mustn't think that! We're not beasts!" he cried out again, and stood up to pace back and forth in the room, from the wall to the window, from the window to the bed.

"My God," the doctor groaned, "this is the most horrible hour of my life."

"Suspicion," the old man said in his bed, and then again, unrelenting: "Suspicion."

Hungertobel stopped next to Barlach's bed. "Please let's forget this conversation, Hans," he said. "We let ourselves go. It's true, we all like to play with possibilities sometimes. It's never a good idea. Let's forget about Emmenberger. The more I look at this picture, the less it looks like him, and I'm not just saying that to wiggle out. He was in Chile and not in Stutthof, and that makes our suspicion meaningless."

"In Chile, in Chile," Barlach said, and his eyes sparkled greedily

for a new adventure. His body stretched, and then he lay motionless and relaxed, with his hands behind his head.

"Your patients are waiting, Samuel," he said after a while. "I don't
want to hold you up any longer. Let's forget our conversation. That's
the best thing to do, I agree."

When Hungertobel turned in the doorway to cast a suspicious
glance at the sick man, the inspector had fallen asleep.

THE ALIBI

The next morning Hungertobel found Barlach studying the *City Gazette*. It was seven thirty, shortly after breakfast. The old man looked surprised, for the doctor had come earlier than usual, at an hour when Barlach was normally asleep again, or at least dozing with his hands behind his head. The doctor also had the impression that Barlach looked peppier than usual. The old vitality seemed to be shining through his narrowed eyelids.

"How are you feeling?" Hungertobel greeted his patient.

"Hopeful," was Barlach's cryptic response.

"I'm earlier than usual, and I'm not here officially," Hungertobel said, stepping up to the bed. "I just wanted to quickly drop off a stack of medical journals: the *Swiss Medical Weekly,* a French one, and especially, since you understand English, some issues of *Lancet,* the famous British medical journal."

"It's sweet of you to assume I'd be interested," Barlach replied without glancing up from his *Gazette,* "but I'm not sure this is appropriate reading matter for me. You know I'm not on good terms with the medical profession."

Hungertobel laughed. "After all we've done for you!"

"Indeed," Barlach said. "That doesn't make it more palatable."

"What are you reading in the *Gazette?*" Hungertobel asked.

"Ads for stamps," the old man replied.

The doctor shook his head. "Nevertheless you will look at these magazines, despite your habit of keeping us doctors at arm's length. I want to prove to you that our talk last night was a lot of foolishness, Hans. You're a criminologist, and I wouldn't put it past you to have our fashionable doctor-suspect arrested out of a clear blue sky, along with his hormones. I don't understand how I could have forgotten it. There's no problem proving that Emmenberger was in Santiago. He sent articles from there to various medical journals, including English and American ones, mainly on the subject of internal secretion, and made a name for himself that way. Even as a student he had a literary flair, his papers were witty and brilliant. You see, he was a good research scientist, hardworking and conscientious. And that's what makes his current turn toward the trendy, if I may call it that, all the more regrettable; because what he's doing now is really a cheap trick, and I'm not just being orthodox when I say that. The last article appeared in *Lancet* in January of forty-five, a few months before he returned to Switzerland. That's certainly proof that our suspicion was a red herring. I give you my solemn vow that I'll never play criminologist again. The man in the picture cannot be Emmenberger, or else the photograph is forged."

"That would be an alibi," Barlach said, folding the *Gazette*. "You can leave the magazines with me."

When Hungertobel came back at ten for his regular visit, the old man was lying in his bed, eagerly reading the magazines.

"So you're interested in medicine after all," the doctor said with surprise as he checked Barlach's pulse.

"You were right," the inspector said, "the articles came from Chile."

Hungertobel was glad and relieved. "You see! And we already had Emmenberger pegged as a mass murderer."

"It's amazing, the advances that have been made in this art," Barlach dryly replied. "Time, my friend, time. I don't need the English journals, but you can leave me the Swiss ones."

"But Emmenberger's articles in *Lancet* are much more important, Hans!" objected Hungertobel, who was already persuaded of his friend's interest in medicine. "Those are the ones you should read."

"But in the *Swiss Medical Weekly* Emmenberger writes in German," Barlach replied somewhat ironically.

"So?" asked the doctor, who understood nothing.

"I mean that I'm intrigued with his style, Samuel, the style of a doctor who was once noted for the elegance of his language and now writes rather clumsily," the old man said cautiously.

"So what?" Hungertobel asked, still unsuspecting, busy with the chart above the bed.

"It's not so easy to furnish an alibi," the inspector said.

"What are you getting at?" the doctor said, dismayed. "Are you still not rid of that suspicion?"

Barlach thoughtfully looked into his friend's appalled face, the noble, wrinkled face of a doctor who had never dealt lightly with his patients and yet knew nothing about human nature. Then he said, "Do you still smoke your 'Little Rose of Sumatra,' Samuel? It would be nice if you offered me one. I imagine lighting one after my boring oatmeal gruel would be a very pleasant experience."

THE DISMISSAL

But before lunch was served, the sick man, who had been reading and rereading an article by Emmenberger on the function of the pancreas, received his first visit since the operation. It was the "boss" who came into the sickroom around eleven and sat down by the old man's bed, without taking off his coat, holding his hat in his hand, and looking vaguely embarrassed. Barlach knew exactly what this visit was about, and the boss knew exactly how things were going for the inspector.

"Well, Inspector," Lutz began, "How are you? There were times when it seemed we had to expect the worst."

"I'm coming along," Barlach replied, folding his hands behind his neck.

"What are you reading?" Lutz asked, looking for an opportunity to avoid the real purpose of his visit. "My, my, Barlach, medical journals!"

The old man was not embarrassed. "It reads like a thriller," he said. "When you're sick, you want to widen your horizons, so you look around for new fields."

Lutz wanted to know how long Barlach was required to remain in bed.

"Two months," the inspector replied. "Two more months they expect me to lie here."

Now the boss could no longer evade the issue. "The age limit . . ." It took him an effort to get the words out. "The age limit, Inspector, you understand, I don't see how we can get around it, we have regulations."

"I understand," the sick man replied. His face betrayed no emotion.

"There's no getting around it," said Lutz. "You need rest and recreation, Inspector, that's what it boils down to."

"That and modern scientific criminology, where you find your criminal like a labeled pot of jam," added the old man by way of correction and inquired who would be his successor.

"Rothlisberger," the boss replied. "He's already substituting for you."

Barlach nodded. "Rothlisberger. He's got five children, he'll be pleased with the pay-raise," he said. "Starting with the New Year?"

"Starting with the New Year."

"Till Friday then," Barlach said, "and from then on, I'll be an exdetective inspector. No more public service, not in Turkey and not in Bern. I'm glad that's over, not because I'll have more time to read Molière and Balzac—though that would be very worthwhile, to be sure—but mainly because, as I see it, there is something very wrong with the way the world is run. I know what goes on. People are always the same, whether they go to the Haga Sophia on Sundays or to the Bern Cathedral. They let the big scoundrels go and lock up the little ones. And there's a whole heap of crimes no one pays any attention to, because they are more esthetic than those blatant murders that get written up in the newspapers, but it all amounts to the same if you care to take a close look and exercise a little imagination. Imagination, that's it! There's many a decent businessman whose lack of imagination permits him to close some crooked deal between cocktails and lunch without ever realizing that he has committed a crime, and neither does anyone else, because imagination is in very short supply. It's carelessness that makes the world a bad place, and from the looks of it, we're going to hell out of sheer carelessness. Next to this threat, Stalin and all the other Josephs look harmless. Public service—for an old bloodhound like me, that's not the right hunting ground any longer. Too much pettiness, too much snooping. But the real prey, the big beasts, the ones most worth hunting because they most deserve it—they're officially off limits, like animals in a zoo."

Doctor Lucius Lutz's face dropped as he heard this oration; he found it embarrassing, and actually he thought it improper not to protest against such a vicious philosophy. But on second thought, the old man was sick and about to retire with a pension, thank God.

"I have to go now," he said, swallowing his anger. "I'm scheduled to meet with the welfare department at eleven thirty."

"The welfare department. They, too, have more dealings with the police than with the department of finance, there's something wrong with that," the inspector remarked. Lutz was already expecting the worst, but to his relief, Barlach was aiming at something else. "You could do me a favor, now that I'm sick and no longer useful."

"Gladly," promised Lutz.

"You see, sir, I need some information. I'm curious by nature, so, for my own private amusement, and to pass the time while I lie here, I've been playing around with criminological puzzles. An old cat can't give up chasing mice. In this issue of *Life* I found a picture of a concentration camp doctor from Stutthof, the name is Nehle. Try to find out, if you don't mind, whether he's still in jail or what became of him. There's an international service for these cases, and it's been free of charge since the SS was declared a criminal organization."

Lutz wrote everything down.

"I'll have my office check into it," he promised, surprised by the old man's whimsical request. Then he got up to leave.

"Good-bye, and get well," he said, shaking the inspector's hand. "You'll have the information by tonight. Then you can puzzle away to your heart's content. Blatter is here, too, he wants to say hello. I'll wait outside in the car."

Blatter came in, and Lutz disappeared.

"Hello, Blatter," Barlach said to the corpulent policeman, who had often been his driver. "I'm glad to see you."

"So am I," said Blatter. "We miss you, Inspector. We miss you everywhere."

"Well, Blatter, now Rothlisberger will take my place, and I imagine he'll change the tune," replied the old man.

"Too bad," said the policeman. "But don't put me on record. I'm sure Rothlisberger will be all right. What's important is that you get better!"

"Blatter, do you know that old bookstore down at the Aare river, the one that belongs to the Jew with the white beard, Feitelbach?"

Blatter nodded. "You mean the one with the stamps in the window, always the same ones?"

"That's the one. Go there this afternoon and tell Feitelbach to send me *Gulliver's Travels*. It's the last service I'll ask of you."

"The book with the dwarves and the giants?" the policeman wondered.

Barlach laughed. "You see, Blatter, I just love fairy tales!"

Something in this laugh struck the policeman as uncanny; but he didn't dare to ask.

THE HUT

That same Wednesday evening, a subordinate of Lutz's called. Hungertobel was sitting at his friend's bedside. He had ordered a cup of coffee, for he had an operation coming up; he wanted to take this opportunity to spend some time with his friend. Now the telephone rang, interrupting their conversation.

Barlach picked up the receiver, said hello, and listened intently. After a while he said, "That's good, Favre. Now just send me the material," and hung up. "Nehle is dead," he said then.

"Thank God!" Hungertobel exclaimed. "We should celebrate that." And he lit up a "Little Rose of Sumatra." "Let's hope the nurse doesn't barge in."

"She didn't much like it at noon," Barlach noted. "But I said you had allowed it. She said that was typical."

"When did Nehle die?" asked the doctor.

"In forty-five, on the tenth of August. He killed himself in a Hamburg hotel, apparently with poison," the inspector replied.

"You see," Hungertobel nodded, "that takes care of whatever was left of your suspicion."

Barlach blinked at the rings and spirals of smoke his friend puffed into the air with evident pleasure. "Nothing is harder to drown than a good suspicion," he finally replied. "It just keeps coming up again."

"You are incorrigible," laughed Hungertobel, who now regarded the whole affair as a harmless joke.

"A detective's prime virtue," retorted the old man. Then he asked, "Samuel, were you and Emmenberger friends?"

"No, we weren't," said Hungertobel, "and as far as I know, he wasn't close to anyone who went to school with him. I've been thinking a lot about that incident with the picture in *Life*, Hans, and I want to tell you how I came to think that this SS-monster could have been Emmenberger; I'm sure you've given that some thought yourself. There's not much to see in the picture, so there must be a reason for my mistake besides a certain resemblance, which I'm sure really exists. It's a story I had put out of my mind, not just because it happened a long time ago, but mainly because it was so terrible; and one tends to forget, or wants to forget, things one finds deeply offensive. I was once present, Hans, when Emmenberger performed an operation without anesthesia, and this was for me like a scene that could happen in hell, if there is such a place."

"There is," Barlach answered quietly. "So there was a time when Emmenberger did something like that?"

"You see," the doctor said, "there was no other way at the time, and the poor bastard who had to go through that operation is still alive. If you see him, he'll swear by all the saints that Emmenberger's the devil incarnate, and that is unfair, because without Emmenberger, he would be dead. But frankly, I can understand him. It was horrible."

"How did it happen?" Barlach asked with intense interest.

Hungertobel drained his cup of coffee. Then he had to light his "Little Rose" again. "It wasn't exactly a feat of magic, to tell you the truth. Our profession is just like any other, there's no magic about it. All he needed was a pocketknife and some courage, and of course knowledge of human anatomy. But who among us young students had the necessary presence of mind?

"There were about five of us, all medical students, climbing up from Kien Valley into the Blümlisalp massif; I don't recall where we were heading, I've never been a great mountain climber, and I'm an even worse geographer. It must have been around 1908, in July. It

was a hot summer, I remember that clearly. We spent the night in an
Alpine hut. It's strange, how this hut stayed with me through all the
years. Sometimes it comes up in my dreams and I wake up bathed
in sweat; but that's never connected to thoughts about what took
place there. I'm sure it was like any other hut in the Alps that's left
vacant through the winter, and the sense of horror attached to it
comes from my imagination. The reason I think so is that I always
see it overgrown with damp moss, and that's not like a real Alpine
hut, it seems to me. Did you ever hear of a 'knacker's hut'? A
knacker, that's someone who turns worn-out farm animals into fer-
tilizer. Anyway, I've come across this word, 'knacker's hut,' and I
always imagined its looking like this particular hut. There were fir
trees standing around it, there was a well near the door. And the
wood of this hut wasn't black, it was sort of white and rotten, with
funguses growing in all the cracks, but that may have been added by
my imagination. So many years lie between now and then, there's
no way to tell where the dream ends and the reality begins. But I still
remember clearly an inexplicable fear that befell me as we approached this hut. We were crossing a stony pasture that wasn't in
use that summer. There was a depression in the meadow, and that's
where the hut stood. I'm convinced we all felt this fear, with the possible exception of Emmenberger. We all stopped talking. The sun set
before we had reached the hut, and that sudden evening atmosphere
had something ghastly about it, because for what seemed an un-
bearably long time, a strange, deep-red light hung over that huge,
empty world of ice and stone, tinting our faces and hands, a deathly
sort of illumination. I imagine that's the kind of light you'd see on a
planet that's farther away from the sun than our own. So we rushed
into the hut as if some awful thing was chasing us. It wasn't hard,
getting in; the door was unlocked. We'd already been told in the Kien
Valley that you could sleep over in this hut. The inside was pathetic,
nothing but a few cots. But in the pale light we noticed some straw
under the roof. A black, crooked ladder led up there, all covered with
last year's dirt and dung. Emmenberger fetched water from the well
outside, with a strange haste, as if he knew what was about to happen. Which is of course impossible. Then we made a fire on the prim-

itive stove. There was a pot there. And then, in that peculiar mood of dread and fatigue that we all seemed unable to shake off, one of us had a near-fatal accident. It was a fat boy from Lucerne, the son of an innkeeper, who was studying medicine like the rest of us—nobody quite knew why, and the year after that, he dropped out of school to take over the family business. Anyway, this rather awkward fellow started climbing up to the loft to bring down some straw, when the ladder collapsed and he hit his throat against a protruding beam, so hard and at such an unfortunate angle that he just lay there moaning. At first we thought he had broken something, but then he started to gasp for breath. We carried him outside and put him on a bench, and there he lay in that terrible light from a sun that had already set, a weird sandy red, refracted from the piled-up clouds overhead. The injured boy was a truly frightening sight to behold. His neck was very swollen, and there were bloody abrasions on it. He was holding his head back, his larynx was jumping fitfully. We noted with horror that his face was getting darker and darker, almost black in that infernal glow on the horizon, and his wide-open eyes were shining like two white, wet pebbles in his face. We struggled desperately with cold compresses. In vain. His throat kept swelling internally, he seemed about to choke. At first he had been driven by a feverish restlessness, but now he was becoming apathetic. His breath hissed, he could no longer speak. This much was clear: he was in mortal danger. And we didn't know what to do. We lacked any sort of experience, and probably knowledge as well. We knew, of course, that an emergency operation might help, but no one dared to think of that. Only Emmenberger understood and didn't hesitate to act. He carefully examined the boy from Lucerne, disinfected his pocketknife in the boiling water on the stove, and then he performed the cut we call a tracheotomy, which sometimes has to be done in an emergency: you set the knife at a transverse angle above the larynx, between the Adam's apple and the cricoid cartilage, and make an incision to create an air passage. It wasn't the operation that was so terrible, Hans, there was no other way to do it, the pocketknife was the right choice. No, the horror was something else, something that took place between those two, in their faces. The injured boy was almost unconscious for lack of air, but still, his eyes were open, in fact wide open, staring, and so he had to be aware of everything that was happening, even though it may have been as in a dream. And when Emmenberger made that incision, my God, Hans, his eyes were wide open then, too, and his face was contorted; it was suddenly as if something devilish was breaking out of those eyes, a sort of tremendous pleasure in hurting someone, or whatever you want to call it. And I was afraid for a moment, maybe just for a second, because that's all the time it took. But I think I was the only one who felt that; because the others didn't dare to watch. I also think that most of what I experienced was in my imagination, that the dark hut and the uncanny light of that evening contributed their part to the illusion. The peculiar thing about that incident, though, is that the fellow from Lucerne never spoke to Emmenberger about that operation that saved his life, that he scarcely even thanked him. A lot of people thought ill of him for that. Emmenberger had everyone's respect after that, he was quite a celebrity. He had a strange career. We thought he would make a big name for himself, but he wasn't interested. He studied a lot, but without any clear pattern. Physics, mathematics, nothing seemed to satisfy him; he was seen at lectures in philosophy and theology, too. He passed his examinations brilliantly, but never opened a practice of his own. He worked as a substitute—for me, too, once, and I have to admit, my patients were enthusiastic about him, except for a few who didn't like him. So he led a restless and lonely life, until he finally emigrated. He published some strange treatises. One about the justification for astrology, for instance, which is one of the most sophistic things I have ever read. As far as I know, he was virtually impossible to get to know and became a cynical, unreliable character, all the more unpleasant because no one was able to fend off his sarcasm. The only thing that surprised us was how he suddenly changed in Chile, that he did such sober, scientific work there; it must have been the climate, or the surroundings. As soon as he was back in Switzerland, he was the same old Emmenberger again, as if nothing had changed."

"I hope you saved the essay on astrology," Barlach said when Hungertobel had finished.

"I'll bring it tomorrow," the doctor replied.

"So that's the story," the inspector said thoughtfully.

"You see," Hungertobel said, "maybe I've spent too much of my life dreaming after all."

"Dreams don't lie," Barlach replied.

"Dreams are the biggest liars of all," Hungertobel said. "But you must excuse me, I have to operate." And he rose from his chair.

Barlach gave him his hand. "I hope it's not a tracheotomy, or whatever you call it."

Hungertobel laughed. "A hernia, Hans. I like that better, even though, frankly, it's more difficult. But now you must rest. There's nothing you need more than twelve hours of sleep."

GULLIVER

But already around midnight the old man woke up when a soft noise came from the window and cold night air streamed into the room.

The inspector didn't turn on the light at once. Instead he wondered what was happening. Finally he guessed that the blinds were being slowly pushed up. The darkness surrounding him was illuminated, the curtains swelled in the half-light, and then he heard the blinds being cautiously lowered. Again the impenetrable darkness of midnight surrounded him, but he sensed that a figure was advancing from the window into the room.

"Finally," Barlach said. "There you are, Gulliver," and turned on his night lamp.

In the room, with the red glow of the lamp upon him, stood a gigantic Jew in an old, spotty, and torn caftan.

The old man lay back in his pillows with his hands behind his head. "I half expected a visit from you tonight. And I could imagine you'd make a good cat burglar, too," he said.

"You are my friend," the intruder replied, "so I came." His head was bald and powerful, his hands were refined, but everything was covered with horrible scars, bearing witness to some inhuman abuse, yet nothing had succeeded in destroying the majesty of this face and this man. The giant stood motionless in the middle of the room, slightly bent, his hands on his thighs. His shadow hovered, ghostlike, on the wall and the curtains, his diamond-clear, lashless eyes gazed on the old man with imperturbable clarity.

"How could you know of my need to be present in Bern?" The words came from a mangled, almost lipless mouth, in an awkward, overly anxious manner of talking, as of one who moves in too many languages and now can't easily find his way in German; but his speech was without accent. "Gulliver leaves no trace," he said after a brief silence. "I work invisibly."

"Everyone leaves a trace," the inspector replied. "Yours is this, I might as well tell you: When you're in Bern, Feitelbach, who hides you, puts an advertisement in the *Gazette* saying that he is selling old books and stamps. I conclude that at such times Feitelbach has some money."

The Jew laughed. "The great art of Commissar Barlach consists in discovering the obvious."

"Now you know your trace," said the old man. "There is nothing worse than a criminologist who spills his secrets."

"I'll leave my trace for Commissar Barlach. Feitelbach is a poor Jew. He will never learn how to make money."

With these words the mighty ghost sat down by the old man's bed. He reached into his caftan and pulled out a large dusty bottle and two small glasses. "Vodka," said the giant. "Let us drink together, Inspector. We have always drunk together."

Barlach sniffed the glass. He liked an occasional schnapps, but he had a bad conscience, for he knew that Dr. Hungertobel would be shocked if he saw all this: the liquor, the Jew, and the time of night, when decent patients should be asleep. He'd have a regular fit: You call this being sick?

"Where's the vodka from?" he asked after taking the first sip. "My, it's good."

"From Russia," Gulliver laughed. "I got it from the Soviets."

"Have you been back in Russia?"

"It's my job, Commissar."

"Inspector," Barlach corrected him. "We don't have commissars in Bern. Don't tell me you wore that awful caftan in the Soviet paradise. Did you ever take it off?"

"I am a Jew and I wear my caftan—I made a vow. This is the national costume of my poor people, and I love it."

"Give me another vodka," Barlach said.

The Jew filled the two glasses.

"I hope climbing the wall wasn't too much for you," Barlach said, frowning. "That's another breach of the law, you know."

"Gulliver can't afford to be seen," the Jew replied.

"But it's dark around eight, and I'm sure they would have let you in for a visit. There are no police here."

"Then I can just as well climb the wall," the giant replied, laughing. "A child could have done it, Commissar. Up the rainspout and along a ledge."

"It's a good thing I'm going into retirement." Barlach shook his head. "I won't have something like you on my conscience any longer. I should have had you locked up years ago. What a catch! I would have been applauded all over Europe."

"You won't do it because you know what I'm fighting for," the Jew replied impassively.

"You could at least get yourself some sort of papers," the old man suggested. "I personally don't care much for that sort of thing, but for God's sake, there has to be some kind of order."

"I am dead," said the Jew. "The Nazis shot me."

Barlach was silent. He knew what the giant was referring to. The light of the lamp encircled the men with a calm glow. Somewhere a bell struck midnight. The Jew refilled the glasses. His eyes gleamed with a strange kind of gaiety.

"When our friends from the SS accidentally left me lying in some miserable lime pit among fifty men of my poor race whom they had shot on a beautiful day in May forty-five—I particularly remember a little white cloud—, and when, hours later, covered with blood, I was able to crawl into a lilac bush that was blooming nearby, so that the troops who shoveled the whole thing under overlooked me, I swore that from that moment on I would lead the existence of an abused and defiled animal, since in this century it appears to have been God's pleasure to have so many of us live like beasts. From then on I lived only in the darkness of graves, staying in cellars and places like that. Only the night has seen my face, and only the stars and the moon have shone on this pitifully torn and tattered caftan. And that's as it should be. The Germans killed me, I saw my death certificate, it came through the *Reichspost* to my former Aryan wife— she's dead now, that too is as it should be—, it was all very correctly filled out, a tribute to the good schools where this nation is raised in the spirit of civilization. Dead is dead, whether you're a Jew or a Christian, forgive the sequence, Commissar. For a dead man there are no papers, you have to admit that, and no borders either. He comes to every country where there are still persecuted and martyred Jews. *Prosit,* Inspector, I drink to our health!"

The two men emptied their glasses; the man in the caftan poured new vodka and said, his eyes tightening into two sparkling slits, "What do you want of me, Commissar Barlach?"

"Inspector," the old man corrected him.

"Commissar," maintained the Jew.

"I need some information," Barlach said.

"Information is good," laughed the giant. "It is worth its weight in gold, if it's solid. Gulliver knows more than the police."

"We'll see. You were in all the concentration camps, you mentioned that once. Though you don't talk much about yourself," Barlach said.

The Jew filled the glasses. "There was a time when I was considered so extremely important that they dragged me from one hell to the next, and there were more than the nine of which Dante sings, who himself was in none. From each one I have brought some hefty scars to this postmortem life that I lead." He stretched out his left hand. It was crippled.

"Maybe you know an SS doctor named Nehle?" the old man asked intently.

The Jew looked thoughtfully at the inspector for a while. "You mean the one from the camp at Stutthof?" he asked then.

"That one," Barlach replied.

The giant gave the old man a quizzical look. "He took his own life in a fleabag hotel in Hamburg on the tenth of August, nineteen forty-five," he said after a while.

"Like hell he knows more than the police," Barlach thought, a little disappointed, and he said, "Was there ever a moment in your career—or whatever one should call it—when you came face to face with Nehle?"

Again the ragged Jew gave the inspector a searching look, and his scar-covered face twisted into a grimace. "Why are you asking me about this perverted beast?" he replied.

Barlach considered telling the Jew about his suspicion, but then he decided not to mention Emmenberger.

"I saw his picture," he said, "and it interests me to know what became of a man like that. I am a sick man, Gulliver, and I'll be lying here for quite a while, you can't keep on reading Molière, sooner or later you start following your own thoughts. So I end up wondering what sort of man he might be, this mass murderer."

"All human beings are the same. Nehle was a human being. So Nehle was like all human beings. It's a nasty syllogism, but it's a truth we can't alter," the giant replied, keeping his eyes fixed on Barlach. Nothing in his powerful face betrayed his thoughts.

"I assume you saw Nehle's picture in *Life*, Commissar," the Jew continued. "It is the only picture that exists of him. They searched all over this beautiful world, but that was the only one they found. Which is embarrassing, because on that famous picture there's not much you can see of the legendary torturer."

"So there's just one picture," Barlach said thoughtfully. "How is that possible?"

"The devil cares better for the elect of his congregation than Heaven does for the saved—he arranged for propitious circumstances," the Jew replied sarcastically. "Nehle's name is not listed in the SS membership files that are kept in Nürnberg these days for the uses of crime-fighters, and it's not listed anywhere else either; he probably wasn't in the SS. The official camp reports from Stutthof to the SS Headquarters never mention his name. It's left out of the personnel registers too. There is something about this man, who has countless victims on his quiet conscience, something legendary and illegal, as if even the Nazis were ashamed of what he did. And yet Nehle lived, and no one ever doubted his existence, not even the most hardboiled atheists; for we all believe readily in a god who contrives the most fiendish tortures. That's why in other camps that were no better than Stutthof, we always talked about him, even though that talk was more like a rumor about one of the most evil and pitiless angels in this paradise of judges and hangmen. And that talk continued even after the fog started to clear. There was no one left from Stutthof whom we could have asked. Stutthof is near Danzig. The few inmates who survived the tortures were mowed down by the SS when the Russians came, and the Russians meted out justice to the guards and hanged them. But Nehle was not among them, Commissar. He must have left the camp earlier."

"But there was a warrant out for him," Barlach said.

The Jew laughed. "For him and a million others, Barlach! The whole German population had turned into a criminal affair. But no one would have remembered Nehle, because no one would have been able to remember him, his crimes would have remained unknown, if at the end of the war *Life* hadn't published this picture you've seen, the picture of a skillful and masterly operation with just one little flaw, that it was performed without anesthesia. Humanity felt an obligatory indignation, and so a search began. Otherwise Nehle could have retired into private life, unmolested, and transformed himself into a harmless country doctor or the head of some highly expensive spa."

"How did *Life* get that picture?" the old man asked innocently.

"The simplest thing in the world," the giant answered calmly. "I gave it to them!"

Barlach shot up to a sitting position and stared, astonished, into the Jew's face. Gulliver knows more than the police after all, he thought, dismayed. This tattered giant, to whom countless Jews owed their lives, himself led an existence in which the most monstrous crimes and vices were threaded together. A judge with his own laws sat before Barlach, a man who acquitted and condemned according to his own discretion, independent of the criminal codes and jurisdictions of the glorious fatherlands of this earth.

"Let us drink vodka," said the Jew, "a stiff drink is always a help.

You have to believe in that, otherwise you'll lose every last sweet illusion on this godforsaken planet."

And he filled the glasses and shouted, "Long live man!" Then he poured down the glass and said, "But how? That is often difficult."

"Don't shout like that," the inspector said, "you'll alarm the night nurse. This is a well-run hospital."

"Christianity, Christianity," said the Jew. "It produced good nurses and some equally competent murderers."

For a moment the old man thought this was enough vodka for an evening, but then he had himself another drink.

For a moment, as the room spun around, Gulliver reminded him of a huge bat. Then the room settled back into a slightly tilted, but reasonably stable, position.

"You knew Nehle," Barlach said.

"I had occasional dealings with him," the giant replied, still occupied with his vodka. Then he began to talk again, but no longer with his former cold, clear voice, but in a strangely singing tone that intensified with inflections of irony or sarcasm, but that also softened at other moments, as if muted. And Barlach understood that everything in this man's speech, including the wildness and the mockery, was just an expression of an immense sorrow over the incomprehensible fall of a once beautiful world created by God. And so this gigantic Ahasuerus sat at midnight next to the old inspector, who lay in his bed close to death listening to the words of this man of sorrows whom the history of our age had shaped into a gloomy, terrifying angel of death.

"It was in December of forty-four," Gulliver reported in his sing-song voice, his pain spreading out on the sea of his drunkenness like a dark sheet of oil, "and still in January of the following year, when the glassy sun of hope was just rising far away on the horizons of Stalingrad and Africa. And yet those months were accursed, Commissar, and for the first time I swore by all our venerable sages and their gray beards that I would not survive. And yet I did survive, thanks to Nehle, about whose life you are so eager to learn. Of this devotee of the medical arts I can tell you that he saved my life by pushing me down into the bottom-most pit of hell and then pulling me up by the hair again, a method that, to my knowledge, only one person survived, namely yours truly, whose curse it is to survive anything; and in the tremendous overflow of my gratitude, I did not hesitate to betray him by taking his picture. In this upside down world there are good deeds that can only be repaid with villainies."

"I don't understand what you're telling me," said the inspector, who wasn't sure how much of what he was hearing had to be attributed to the effects of vodka.

The giant laughed and drew a second bottle out of his caftan. "Forgive me," he said, "I'm making long sentences, but my torments were longer. What I'm trying to say is simple: Nehle operated on me. Without anesthesia. I was the recipient of this extraordinary honor. Forgive me again, Commissar, but I have to drink vodka and drink it like water when I think back on that, because it was awful."

"Damn," Barlach exclaimed, and then again into the silence of the hospital, "Damn." He had raised himself up to a half-sitting position. Mechanically he held out his empty glass to the monster by his bedside.

"All it takes to hear this story is a little nerve; less nerve than it did to live through it," continued the Jew in his old musty caftan in a singing tone. "It's time to forget all these things, they say, and not just in Germany; there's cruelty in Russia too, and there are sadists everywhere; but I don't want to forget anything, and not just because I am a Jew—six million of my people the Germans killed, six million!—; no, it's because I am still a human being, even though I live in basements and cellars with the rats! I refuse to make a distinction between peoples, I refuse to speak of good and bad nations; but I do have to make one distinction between human beings, this was beaten into me, and from the first blow that cut into my flesh I distinguished between the torturers and the tortured. I don't deduct the new cruelties of other guards in other countries from the bill I present to the Nazis, I add them to it. I take the liberty of not distinguishing among those who torture. They all have the same eyes. If there is a God, Commissar, and my desecrated heart hopes for nothing more, then there are no nations in his sight, but only human beings, and he will judge each one by the measure of his crime and the measure of his justice. Christian, Christian, listen to the tale of a Jew whose people crucified your savior and who was then nailed to the cross with his people by the Christians: There I lay in the agony of my flesh and my soul in the concentration camp of Stutthof, in a death camp, as they are called, near the venerable city of Danzig, for whose sake this criminal war was unleashed, and there, radical measures were taken. Jehovah was far away, preoccupied with other worlds, or maybe some theological problem was claiming his sublime intelligence, in any case his people were enthusiastically hounded to death, gassed or shot, depending on the mood of the SS, or on the weather: the east wind meant hangings, and the west wind meant now was the time to set dogs on Judah. And so we had this Dr. Nehle, whose fate you are so eager to know, a man of the civilized world. He was one of those camp doctors that proliferated like tumors in every camp: blowflies devoted to mass murder with scientific zeal, who injected prisoners by the hundreds with air, phenol, carbolic acid, and whatever else was available between heaven and earth for this infernal entertainment, or who, if the need arose, performed their experiments on human beings without anesthesia—a necessity, they said, because their fat Reichsmarschall had forbidden vivisection of animals. So Nehle was not alone.— And now I shall have to speak of him. In the course of my travels through the various camps I took a close look at the torturers, and you might say I know the type. Nehle excelled in his field in many ways. He did not participate in the cruelties the others indulged in. I have to admit that he helped the prisoners as far as possible, and to the extent that such help could serve any purpose in a camp that was designed to destroy everyone. He was a monster in a completely different sense than the other doctors, Commissar. His experiments were not outstandingly cruel in the way of physical torture; there were others under whose care Jews died of pain, and not of their medical art. His devilry was that he did all this with the consent of his victims. Improbable as it may be, Nehle only operated on Jews who volunteered, who knew exactly what awaited them, who even, this was his condition, had to watch operations to see the full horror of the torture before they could give their consent to suffer through the same thing."

"How was this possible?" Barlach asked breathlessly.

"Hope," laughed the giant, and his chest rose and fell. "Hope, Christian." His eyes sparkled with an inscrutable, wild depth, like an animal's, the scars on his face stood out, his hands lay like huge paws on Barlach's blanket, his mangled mouth greedily sucked new quantities of vodka into his brutalized body and moaned with a world-weary sorrow. "Faith, hope, and charity, these three, as it says so beautifully in Corinthians, thirteen. But hope is the toughest of them all, that's written right into this Jew's flesh with red letters. Faith and charity, *they* went to the devil in Stutthof, but hope, hope remained, and with it *you* went to the devil. Hope, hope! Nehle had hope in his pocket, all fit and ready, and he offered it to anyone who wanted it, and there were many who did. It's not to be believed, Commissar, but hundreds allowed themselves to be operated by Nehle without anesthesia after standing by, shivering and pale as death, as their predecessor screamed out his life on the operation table, and while they could still say no, all for the mere hope of acquiring the freedom Nehle promised. Freedom! How great must be man's love of freedom, that he should willingly suffer anything for it, even the flaming depths of hell in Stutthof, just to embrace that pitiful bastard freedom offered him there. Sometimes freedom is a whore, sometimes a saint, she's different for each person, one thing for a worker and another for a priest, another yet for a banker, and different again for a poor Jew in a death camp like Auschwitz, Lublin, Maidanek, Natzweiler, and Stutthof: There, freedom was everything that was outside that camp, but not God's beautiful world, oh no, in our boundless modesty all we hoped for was to be transferred back to so pleasant a place as Buchenwald or Dachau, which *now* looked like golden freedom itself, a camp where you didn't run the danger of being gassed but just of being beaten to death, where you had a thousandth of a thousandth particle of hope to be saved by some improbable accident, as against the absolute certainty of death in the extermination camps. My God, Commissar, let us fight for a world where freedom means the same for every-one, where no one has to be ashamed of his freedom! It's laughable: the hope of getting into another concentration camp drove masses of people, or let's say large numbers of them, onto Nehle's flaying-bench; it is laughable;" (and here the Jew actually broke out into a laugh of derision, rage, and despair) "and I, too, Christian, I, too, lay down on the bloody trestle, saw Nehle's knives and pliers move shadowlike in the spotlight above me, and then sank down into the infinite gradations of agony, those brilliant rooms where we see our-selves mirrored in endless revelations of pain! I, too, went to him in the hope of escaping this camp after all, this place cursed by God. Because, you see, this marvelous psychologist Nehle had proven himself helpful and reliable in other respects, so we believed him on this score, that's how people are, we always believe in a miracle when the need is greatest. Verily, verily, he kept his word! When I, the only one, survived a senseless stomach resection, he had me nursed to health and sent back to Buchenwald. That was in the first days of February. However, I never reached Buchenwald, because after end-less transports, there came that beautiful May day near the town of Eisleben, when I ended up hiding inside a blooming lilac bush. These are the deeds of the far-traveled man sitting before you at your bed, Commissar, his sufferings and navigations through the bloody oceans of absurdity of this age. And still the wreck of my body and soul is being swept along through the whirls of our time, which are swallowing millions and millions into their depths, guilty and in-nocent alike. But now the second bottle of vodka is empty, and Ahasuerus must take the highway along the ledge and down the rainspout and back to the damp cellar in Feitelbach's house."

Gulliver rose to his feet, his shadow shrouded half the room in darkness. But the old man did not let him go yet.

"What sort of man was Nehle?" he asked, and his voice was scarcely more than a whisper.

"Christian," said the Jew, who had hidden the bottles and the glasses in his dirty caftan again. "Who could answer your question? Nehle is dead, he just took his own life, his secret is with God, who reigns over heaven and hell, and God will no longer give out his secrets, not even to the theologians. It is deadly to search where there is only death. How often I have tried to slip behind the mask of this doctor with whom no conversation was possible, who was not approachable by the SS or any of the other doctors, let alone by an inmate! How often I tried to fathom what went on behind his glittering spectacles! What was a poor Jew like myself supposed to do, if he never saw his tormentor except with his face half covered and in a white smock? For the picture I took of Nehle, at extreme risk to my life—there was nothing more dangerous in a concentration camp than to make a photograph—showed him as he always was: a haggard figure dressed in white, slightly stooped and silent, as if afraid to be contaminated, walking about in these barracks full of gruesome woe and misery. He was intent on being careful, I believe. He must have always expected that some day the whole infernal specter of the concentration camps would disappear—in order to break out anew from the depths of human instinct like a pestilence with new tormentors and other political systems. So he must have been always preparing for his flight into private life, as if his stint in hell was just a temporary job. It was on this assumption that I calculated my blow, Commissar, and I aimed it well: When the picture appeared in *Life,* Nehle shot himself; it was enough that the world knew his name, Commissar, for a man who is cautious conceals his name!" Those were the last words the old man heard from Gulliver. They resounded fearfully in his ear, like the dull clang of a brass bell, ". . . his name!"

Now the vodka took its effect. It seemed to the sick man as if the curtains over there by the window swelled like the sails of a vanishing ship, as if he could hear the rattling of a venetian blind; then, even less distinctly, as if a huge, massive body was descending into the night; but when the immense profusion of stars burst through the gaping wound of the open window, a wild defiance rose up in him, a determination to fight in *this* world for another, better world, even with this miserable body, on which cancer was gnawing with a steady, unstoppable greed, a body that had been given another year to live and no more. As the vodka started to burn like fire in his bowels, a song broke out of him, the "Berner March." He bellowed it into the silence of the hospital, rousing the other patients from their sleep. He could think of nothing stronger; but when the distressed nurse came rushing in, he was already asleep.

THE SPECULATION

The next morning, a Thursday, Barlach awoke, as was to be expected, around twelve, shortly before lunch was served. His head seemed a little heavy, but otherwise he felt better than he had in a long time, and he thought to himself that a swig of booze now and then was still the best thing, especially when you were sick in bed and not allowed to drink. There was mail on his night table; Lutz had sent news about Nehle. The police were well organized these days, you really couldn't fault them, especially when you were about to receive your pension, as would be the case day after tomorrow, thank God; back in the old days, in Constantinople, it sometimes took months for information to reach you. But before the old man could get to his reading, the nurse brought his meal. It was Lina, his favorite among the nurses, but she seemed reserved today, not her usual self. Something was amiss, he could tell. Probably they had found out about last night, though he couldn't imagine how. He had the impression of having sung the "Berner March" at the end, after Gulliver had left, but this had to be an illusion, he wasn't the least bit patriotic. Damn it, he thought, if only I could remember! The old man looked suspiciously around the room while fishing around in his oatmeal gruel. (Always oatmeal gruel!) On the washstand stood some bottles and medicines that hadn't been there before. What was that supposed to mean? There was something fishy about the whole thing. Besides, every ten minutes a different nurse would come in to fetch something, look for something, bring something; one of them was giggling outside in the hallway, he could hear it clearly. He didn't dare ask for Hungertobel, and it was quite all right with him that he would be gone till evening, since he had his practice in the city during noon hours. Barlach gloomily swallowed his cream of wheat with apple sauce (no change in that either), but then he was surprised to be served a strong coffee with sugar for dessert— special instructions from Dr. Hungertobel, as the nurse reproachfully put it. This had never happened before. He enjoyed the coffee, and it lifted his spirits. Then he immersed himself in the dossier. That seemed the smartest thing to do, but to his surprise, Hungertobel came already at one, with an alarmed look on his face, as the old man noted with an imperceptible movement of his eyes, though he still seemed absorbed in his papers.

"Hans," Hungertobel said, resolutely stepping up to the bed, "for God's sake, what happened? I could swear, and so could all the nurses, that you were totally drunk!"

"Hm," said the old man, glancing up from his dossier. And then he said, "Is that so?"

"Yes indeed," Hungertobel replied, "it's written all over you. I tried to wake you up all morning."

"I'm sorry to hear that," the inspector said.

"It's practically impossible that you drank alcohol, unless you swallowed the bottle too!" the doctor exclaimed in desperation.

"I'd say so," the old man grinned.

"It's a mystery," Hungertobel said, wiping his glasses. He did that whenever he was upset.

"Dear Samuel," the inspector said, "I'm sure it's not easy to give room and board to a criminologist, and if you believe I'm a secret lush, I'll have to accept that. I have only one request: call the Sonnenstein clinic in Zürich and have me signed up as a freshly operated, bedridden, but rich patient named Blaise Kramer."

"You want to go to Emmenberger?" Hungertobel asked, and sat down in dismay.

"Of course," Barlach replied.

"Hans," Hungertobel said, "I don't understand you. Nehle is dead."

"One Nehle is dead," the old man corrected him. "Now we have to find out which one."

"For God's sake," the doctor asked breathlessly, "are there two Nehles?"

Barlach picked up the dossier. "Let's look at the case together," he continued calmly, "and let's see what strikes our eyes. You'll notice that our art is comprised of some mathematics and a lot of imagination."

"I don't understand a thing," Hungertobel moaned, "I've been in the dark all morning."

"I'm reading the physical description," the inspector continued. "Tall, haggard figure; gray hair, formerly brown-red; greenish-gray eyes; protruding ears; the face slim and pale, with bags under the eyes; healthy teeth. Special marks: scar on right eyebrow."

"That's him to a T," said Hungertobel.

"Who?" asked Barlach.

"Emmenberger," replied the doctor. "I recognized him from the description."

"But this is the police's description of Nehle, the man who was found dead in Hamburg," Barlach retorted.

"All the more natural that I mistook one man for the other," Hungertobel remarked with satisfaction. "Any one of us can resemble a murderer. My mistake has found the simplest explanation in the world—obviously!"

"That's one conclusion," said the inspector. "But it's not the only possible one. There are other possibilities—not as compelling at first glance, but still, they'll have to be considered as 'maybes.' One possible conclusion, for instance, might be that it wasn't Emmenberger who was in Chile, but Nehle under his name, while Emmenberger was in Stutthof under Nehle's name."

"Not a very likely conclusion," Hungertobel said.

"Certainly," Barlach replied, "but admissible. We have to consider all possibilities."

"Good lord, where would that get us!" the doctor protested.

"That would mean that Emmenberger killed himself in Hamburg and that the doctor who is practicing in the Sonnenstein clinic is Nehle."

"Have you seen Emmenberger since he came back from Chile?" the old man interjected.

"Just in passing," Hungertobel replied. He put his hand on his head; the question had taken him aback. He had finally put his glasses back on again.

"You see," the inspector continued, "the possibility exists! Another solution is possible: The dead man in Hamburg is Nehle returned from Chile, while Emmenberger, who was known in Stutthof as Nehle, returned to Switzerland."

"If that were the case, we would have to presume a crime," Hungertobel said, shaking his head. "There's no other way to maintain this strange hypothesis."

"Correct, Samuel!" the inspector nodded. "We would have to assume that Nehle was killed by Emmenberger."

"We could just as well assume the opposite: Nehle killed Emmenberger. You are obviously free to imagine anything you want."

"This hypothesis is also correct," Barlach said. "We may presume it as possible, at least at the present stage of our speculations."

"That's a lot of nonsense," said the doctor.

"Possibly," Barlach replied enigmatically.

Hungertobel protested vigorously: "This is much too simplistic. The way you juggle with reality, you can prove anything you want! With this method just about anything can be put in question!"

"That is the duty of a criminologist," the old man replied, "to reality in question. That's just the way it is. In this regard we have to proceed like philosophers, of whom it is said that they start by doubting everything and then proceed to elaborate beautiful speculations about the art of dying and life after death—except we're probably even more useless than they are. You and I have set up a number of hypotheses. All of them are possible. That is the first step. The next one will be to identify those that are probable. Possible and probable are not the same thing; what is possible need not be probable, not at all. So we have to examine the degree of probability in our hypotheses. We have two persons, two doctors: on the one hand Nehle, a criminal, and on the other your former fellow student, Emmenberger, the director of the Sonnenstein clinic in Zürich. What we have essentially done is set up two hypotheses. Both are possible. At first glance the degree of their probability is far from equal. One hypothesis states that there is no connection between Emmenberger and Nehle, and is probable; the second one presumes a connection and is less probable."

"Exactly," Hungertobel interjected, "that's what I've been saying all along."

"Dear Samuel," Barlach replied, "unfortunately, I am a criminologist, and that obliges me to detect crimes in the web of human relationships. The first hypothesis—the one proposing that there is no connection between Nehle and Emmenberger—doesn't interest me. Nehle is dead and there is nothing to charge Emmenberger with. But my profession forces me to examine the second, less probable hypothesis more closely. What is probable about it? The idea is that Nehle and Emmenberger switched roles and identities: that Emmenberger was in Stutthof as Nehle and performed operations without anesthesia on the inmates, and that Nehle lived in Chile as Emmenberger and from there sent articles and reports to medical journals; not to mention all the rest, Nehle's death in Hamburg and Emmenberger's residence in Zürich. This hypothesis looks rather fantastical, we can admit that for the time being. However, it is still within the realm of possibility insofar as Emmenberger and Nehle are not only both doctors but also resemble each other. And here is a factor requiring some closer attention. It is the first fact we've come across in this tangle of possibilities and probabilities. Let us examine this fact. How do these two men resemble each other? Resemblance is not very unusual. Great resemblance is rarer, and rarest of all, I would think, are cases where two people resemble each other even in accidental details, in distinguishing marks that don't stem from nature but from a specific event. That is the case here. Not only do they both have the same hair and eye color, similar facial features, the same build, and so on, they also both have the same peculiar scar on the right eyebrow."

"Well, that's a coincidence," said the doctor.

"Or skill," the old man replied. "You once operated on Emmenberger's eyebrow. What was wrong with him?"

"The scar comes from an operation that has to be performed in case of a very severe sinus infection," Hungertobel replied. "You make the cut in the eyebrow, to hide the scar. I obviously didn't do a good job in Emmenberger's case. Bad luck, I'd say—because usually I operate very accurately. A decent surgeon shouldn't leave such a prominent scar; and later it turned out a part of his eyebrow was missing."

"Is this a common operation?" the inspector asked.

"Well, not exactly," Hungertobel replied. "Normally, sinusitis gets treated before surgery becomes necessary."

"You see," said Barlach, "there's the peculiar thing: This rather rare operation was performed on Nehle as well as Emmenberger; he too has a gap in his eyebrow, and according to the police record, it's in the same spot: that corpse in Hamburg was carefully examined. Did Emmenberger have a scald mark about as wide as a hand on his lower left arm?"

"How did you figure that out?" Hungertobel was surprised. "Emmenberger once had an accident during a chemical experiment."

"That same scar was found on the corpse in Hamburg," Barlach said with satisfaction. "Does Emmenberger still have those marks today? It would be important to know this—you said you saw him briefly."

"Last summer in Ascona," the doctor replied. "Emmenberger still had both scars, I noticed that right away. He was his old self altogether. He made a few nasty remarks and otherwise hardly recognized me."

"Ah," said the inspector, "so he seemed not to recognize you, or hardly. You see, the resemblance goes so far that we're no longer quite sure who's who. We are forced to presume one of two things: a rare and strange coincidence, or some artful trick. Probably the similarity between the two wasn't as great as we now believe. Two people can look similar in their passports and official papers without being readily confused for one another. But when the resemblance involves such accidental things, the chances of one man imperson-ating the other are greatly increased. Then the device of a make-believe operation and an artificially induced accident would have the purpose of turning resemblance into sameness. However, we can only voice assumptions at this stage of our investigation; but you have to admit that this kind of resemblance makes our second hy-pothesis more probable."

"Is there no other picture of Nehle besides the one in *Life?*" Hungertobel asked.

"Three pictures from the Hamburg crime squad," the inspector replied, took the pictures from the folder, and gave them to his friend. "They show a dead man."

"There's not much left to recognize," Hungertobel said after a while, disappointed. His voice was quivering. "There really may be a strong resemblance. I could even imagine Emmenberger looking like this in death. How did Nehle kill himself?"

The old man directed a thoughtful, lowering look at the doctor, who sat helplessly by his bed in his white smock and had forgotten everything, Barlach's drunkenness and the waiting patients. "With cyanide," the inspector finally said. "Like most Nazis."

"In what form?"

"He bit on a capsule and swallowed it."

"On an empty stomach?"

"That's what they determined."

"That works on the spot," Hungertobel said, "and on these pic-tures it looks as if Nehle saw something horrible before his death." The two men fell silent.

Finally the inspector said, "Let's go on, even though Nehle's death presents a puzzle; we have to investigate the other suspicious factors."

"I don't understand how you can speak of further suspicious fac-tors," Hungertobel said, at once surprised and depressed. "That's going too far."

"Oh no," said Barlach. "First there's your experience as a stu-dent. I'll touch on it only briefly. It helps me insofar as it gives me a psychological clue as to *why* Emmenberger *might* have been capable of the acts we are forced to presume he committed *if* he was in Stutthof. But I'm getting to another, more important fact: I am here in possession of the curriculum vitae of the man we know by the name of Nehle. His background is dismal. He was born in 1890, so he's three years younger than Emmenberger. He's from Berlin. His father is unknown, his mother was a maid who left her illegitimate son with his grandparents, led a vagrant existence, eventually wound up in a house of correction, and then disappeared. The grandfather worked with the Borsig Corporation. He, too, was born out of wedlock. He came to Berlin from Bavaria when he was young. The grandmother was Polish. Nehle went to public school and entered the army at fourteen, was in the infantry till he was fifteen, and was then transferred to the medical corps, upon request of a medical officer. Here an irresistible attraction to the medical profession seems to have awakened in him; he was decorated with the Iron Cross for successfully carrying out emergency operations. After the war he worked as an orderly in various mental institutions and hospitals, and studied for his high school degree in his spare time, so he could go on to medical college. But he flunked twice. He failed in Greek and Latin and in mathematics. The man seems to have had no talent for anything except medicine. Then he became a naturopath and miracle doctor with clients from every social stratum, got into conflict with the law, was punished with a rather small fine because, in the court's opinion, his medical knowledge was 'astonishing.' Petitions were drafted, the newspapers defended him. In vain. Then all the hubbub subsides. Since he never gave up his illegal practices, the authorities decided to look the other way. In the thirties, Nehle doctored around in Silesia, Westphalia, Bavaria, and Hesse. Then, after twenty years, the big turning point: he passes his matriculation exams in 1938. (Emmenberger emigrated from Germany to Chile in 1937!) Nehle's performance in mathematics and in Greek and Latin was brilliant. The university passes a decree allowing him to take the state boards without a course of study. He passes this exam as brilliantly as the previous one, and receives his doctor's diploma. But then, to everyone's amazement, he disappears to work as a doctor in the concentration camps."

"My God," said Hungertobel, "what sort of conclusion are you aiming at now?"

"Simple," Barlach said, not without mockery. "Let's look at these articles by Emmenberger that appeared in the *Swiss Medical Weekly* and were written in Chile. These, too, add up to a fact that cannot be ignored, and that we have to examine. You say these articles are scientifically remarkable. I'm willing to believe that. But what I can't believe is that they were written by a man who had command of a distinguished literary style, as you have said of Emmenberger. It's hard to imagine a more awkward use of language."

"A scientific treatise is not a poem," the doctor protested. "Kant, too, wrote in a complicated way."

"Leave Kant out of this," the old man grumbled. "His writing is difficult, but not bad. The author of these contributions from Chile, however, writes not just awkwardly, but ungrammatically. The man obviously didn't know the difference between the dative and the accusative case, a fairly common problem among Berliners. It's peculiar, too, that he often confuses Greek and Latin, as if he didn't know a thing about either language; for instance, in number fifteen from the year forty-two, the word *gastrolysis.*"

There was deadly silence in the room.

For minutes.

Then Hungertobel lit up a "Little Rose of Sumatra."

"In short, you believe that Nehle wrote this treatise?" he finally asked.

"I consider it probable," the inspector calmly replied.

"I have no arguments left," the doctor said gloomily. "You have proved the truth."

"Let's not exaggerate," said the old man, closing the folder on his blanket. "All I have proved is the probability of my hypotheses. The probable is not necessarily the real. If I say it will probably rain tomorrow, it doesn't mean it will rain. In this world, idea and reality are not identical. If they were, we'd have it a lot easier, Samuel. Between idea and reality we still have the adventure of this existence, and by God, that's a challenge."

"It makes no sense," Hungertobel moaned, looking helplessly at his friend, who was lying with his hands behind his head, motionless, as usual. "You're running a terrible risk if your speculation is right, because that would mean Emmenberger is a devil!"

"I know," the inspector nodded.

"It doesn't make sense," the doctor repeated softly, almost whispering.

"Justice always makes sense," Barlach insisted. "Arrange for me to see Emmenberger. I want to go tomorrow."

"On New Year's Eve?" Hungertobel sprang to his feet.

"Yes," the old man replied, "on New Year's eve." And then his eyes glittered with mockery. "Did you bring Emmenberger's treatise on astrology?"

"Certainly," stammered the doctor.

Barlach laughed. "Then hand it over. I'm curious to see if there's anything about *my* star in there. Maybe I have a chance after all."

ANOTHER VISIT

The terrifying old man, who spent the rest of the afternoon laboriously filling a long sheet of paper with his small script and making phone calls to his bank and a notary, this sick man with the inscrutable demeanor of a stone idol, to whom the nurses came with more and more reluctance and who spun his threads with unshakable calm, like a gigantic spider, imperturbably joining one corollary to the next, received another visitor in the evening, shortly after Hungertobel had informed him that he could enter the Sonnenstein clinic on New Year's Eve. It was hard to tell whether the short, skinny fellow with the long neck had come voluntarily or whether Barlach had summoned him. The pockets of his open raincoat were stuffed with newspapers. More newspapers were stuck in the pockets of the torn gray clothes he wore under his coat. A lemon-colored spotty silk scarf was wound around his dirty neck, a beret clung to his bald head. His eyes sparkled under bushy brows, the strong hooked nose seemed too large for this dwarfish man, and the mouth underneath was pathetically sunken, for he had lost his teeth. He was talking to himself, in verse, it seemed, and in between, separate words appeared like islands in the drift, such as "trolley bus . . . traffic police . . ."—things he seemed to find boundlessly annoying. He was swinging and shaking a cane in a wild and erratic fashion. This cane was quite out of keeping with his shabby clothes: it was elegant, if old-fashioned, with a silver handle, obviously made in another century. At the main entrance he collided with a nurse, bowed, stammered an effusive apology, wandered off into the maternity ward and got hopelessly lost there, nearly burst into the delivery room, which was bustling with activity, was chased away by a doctor, stumbled over one of the vases full of carnations that stand in front of all the doors there. Finally he was led into the new hospital wing (after being captured like a frightened animal), but just before he stepped into the old man's room, his cane got between his legs and he slid down half the corridor and slammed against a door behind which an extremely ill man was lying.

"These traffic policemen!" the visitor exclaimed when he finally stood in front of Barlach's bed. (Praise the Lord! thought the student nurse who had accompanied him.) "Wherever you look, they're standing around. A whole city full of traffic police!"

For safety's sake, the inspector took up his excited visitor's topic. "True, Fortschig, but there is a need for traffic police. There has to be order in the flow of traffic, otherwise there'll be even more deaths than we already have."

"Order in the flow of traffic!" Fortschig cried with his squeaky voice. "Great. I'm all for it. But for this you don't need a special police force, what you need is more faith in the decency of people. The whole city of Bern has been turned into one big encampment for the traffic police, it's no wonder everyone using the streets is going crazy. But that's what Bern has always been, a nice little hole in the wall for policemen to nest in. This place has been one infestation of tyranny from the beginning. Lessing already wanted to write a tragedy about Bern when he heard of Henzi's miserable death. A pity he didn't write it! Fifty years I've been living in this fat sleepy hick town of a capital, I can't begin to tell you what it means for a writer, a man of words (not of letters!), to starve and vegetate in this place where all you get for mental food is the weekend book review section in the *Bund*. It's awful, really awful! For fifty years I've been closing my eyes as I walk through Bern, I was already doing that in my stroller. I didn't want to see this wretched town where my father was going to the dogs as some useless adjunct, and now that I open my eyes, what do I see? Traffic policemen, wherever I look."

"Fortschig," the old man said energetically, "We're not here to talk about the traffic police," and he fixed a stern gaze on the squalid, moldy little man who had sat down on a chair and was swaying to and fro with huge owl eyes, shaken by misery.

"I don't know what's the matter with you," the old man continued. "Damn it, Fortschig, you've got brains, you used to be a hell of a guy, and the *Apfelschuss* you published was a good newspaper, even though it was small; but now you're filling it with all sorts of indifferent stuff like traffic police, trolley buses, dogs, stamp collectors, ballpoint pens, radio programs, theater gossip, tram tickets, movie ads, councilmen, and card games. The energy and the pathos with which you go tilting at these things—each time like a scene from Schiller's *Wilhelm Tell*—is worthy of better causes, God knows."

"Inspector!" the visitor squawked. "Inspector! Beware of the sin of offending against a poet, a writer who has the infinite bad luck of having to live in Switzerland and, what is ten times worse, to live *off* Switzerland."

"Now, now," Barlach tried to appease him, but Fortschig became wilder and wilder.

"*Now, now!*" he screamed and leaped up from his chair, ran to the window, from there to the door and back again, to and fro, like a pendulum. "*Now, now,* that's easy to say. But what does it excuse? Nothing! By God, nothing! All right, I've become a ridiculous figure, almost like one of our Habakuks, Theobalds, Eustaches and Moustaches, or whatever they call themselves, whose adventures with collar buttons, wives, and razor blades fill the columns of our dear boring dailies—in the entertainment section, to be sure; but tell me someone who hasn't sunk to that level in this country, where poets still muse about the stirrings of the soul while the world all around us comes down with a crash! Inspector, Inspector, you have no idea what it's taken out of me, just trying to make a decent living with my typewriter. I earn less than your average villager on the dole. I've had to give up one project after another, one hope after another, the best plays, the most fiery poems, the most sublime stories! Houses of cards, that's all it amounted to, houses of cards! Switzerland turned me into a fool, a space cadet, a Don Quixote who fights against windmills and herds of sheep. You're supposed to stand up for freedom and justice and all those other nice little items the fatherland puts up for sale, and show proper respect to a society that forces you to live like a bum and a beggar if you dedicate yourself to the mind instead of to business. These people want to enjoy life, but refuse to share the tiniest fraction of this pleasure, not a crumb and not a penny, and just as, in the Thousand Year Reich, they'd cock their revolvers the moment they heard the word culture, here they tuck away their wallets."

"Fortschig," Barlach said sternly, "I'm glad you're bringing up Don Quixote, because that's a favorite subject of mine. Every one of us would be a Don Quixote, if he had his heart in the right place and just a grain of common sense in his head. But we're not up against windmills, my friend, like that shabby old knight in his tin suit of armor, we have dangerous giants to contend with, monsters of brutality and cunning, and sometimes genuine dinosaurs, the kind who have always had brains like sparrows: these creatures exist, not in fairy tales or in our imagination, but in reality. And that is our job, to fight inhumanity in all its forms and under any circumstances. But it's important *how* we fight, and that we do it with some intelligence. Fighting evil should not be like playing with fire. But that is what you are doing, Fortschig, playing with fire, because you are waging the good fight foolishly, like a fireman who squirts oil at the flames instead of water. Anyone reading the magazine you publish, this pitiful little paper, and taking it at its word, would have to conclude that all of Switzerland should be abolished. I know very well this country's not perfect—to put it very mildly!—and frankly it's turned my hair gray; but then to throw everything into the fire, as if we were living in Sodom and Gomorrha, that's not right, and it's not good manners either. You almost act as if you're ashamed of still loving this country. I don't like that, Fortschig. No one should be ashamed of his love, and love of one's country is still a good ve—only it has to be stern and critical, otherwise it's just idolatry. So when you find dirty spots on your fatherland, you should start sweeping and scrubbing; like Hercules when he cleaned out Augeas' stable—of all his ten labors, that one's my favorite; but to tear the whole house down is senseless and not very smart; because it's hard to build a new house in this poor wounded world; it takes more than a generation to do that, and when it's finally built, it won't be better than the old one. What's important is that it's possible to tell the truth, and to fight for it without being put in a madhouse. This possibility exists in Switzerland, so let's admit it and be thankful that we don't have to be afraid of senators and state councillors, or whatever they're called. True, there are more than a few who are forced to wear rags and live somewhat uncomfortably from one day to the next. That is an outrage, I won't deny it. But a true Don Quixote is proud of his skimpy armor. The struggle against stupidity and egotism has always been difficult and costly, it has always entailed poverty and humiliation; but it is a holy struggle, and it should be fought with dignity and not with wails and lamenting. But you thunder and curse into the ears of our good Berner folk what an unjust fate you are suffering among them, and you wish for the nearest comet-tail to whip our old city to smithereens. Fortschig, Fortschig, you are subverting your fight with petty motives. You can't talk about justice with a capital J and have an eye on your breadbasket at the same time. Stop complaining about your own misfortune and the torn pants you have to wear, give up this petty sniping at worthless things. For God's sake, our world has bigger problems than the traffic police."

The scrawny little man crawled back into the armchair, pulled in his long neck and drew up his legs, the picture of misery. His beret fell behind the chair, and the lemon-yellow scarf hung sadly on his concave chest.

"Inspector," he whined, "you are stern with me, like Moses or Isaiah with the people of Israel, and I know how right you are; but I haven't had a hot meal in four days, I don't even have money for cigarettes."

"I thought you were eating at the Leibundguts," the old man said, frowning and suddenly a little embarrassed.

"I had a fight with Mrs. Leibundgut about Goethe's *Faust*," the writer whined. "She is in favor of the second part and I am against it. So she stopped inviting me. Her husband wrote to me. He says the second part of Faust is his wife's holy of holies, and that he can no longer do anything for me."

Barlach felt sorry for the poor fellow. "Maybe I've been too tough on him," he thought. Finally, out of sheer discomfort, he grumbled, "What the hell does the wife of the president of a chocolate company have to do with Goethe? And whom are they inviting now? That tennis teacher again?"

"Botzinger," Fortschig replied meekly.

"Well, at least *he'll* have a decent meal every three days for a couple of months," the old man said, feeling somewhat reconciled. "A good musician. Except for his compositions. I've heard some godawful noises in my time, especially in Constantinople, you'd think I'd developed an ear for cacophony, but this is beyond me. But no matter. However, I'm sure he'll end up disagreeing with the lady of the house about Beethoven's Ninth. And then she'll go back to the tennis teacher. They're easier to dominate intellectually. As for you, Fortschig, I'll recommend you to the Grollbachs, you know, the ones from the Grollbach-Kuhne clothing store; their cooking is good, a little too greasy. I think you'll last longer there than with the Leibundguts. Grollbach is unliterary and has no interest either in Faust or in Goethe."

"And his wife?" Fortschig anxiously asked.

"Stone deaf," the inspector said. "Luckily for you, Fortschig. And take that little brown cigar over there on the night table. A 'Little Rose.' Dr. Hungertobel left it on purpose, you can smoke in this room with impunity."

With a good deal of fuss and circumstance, Fortschig lit the cigar.

"Would you like to go to Paris for ten days?" Barlach casually asked.

"To Paris?" the little man screamed, leaping up from his chair. "By my soul, if I have one, did you say Paris? I, who worship French literature like nobody else? With the next train!"

Fortschig's surprise and delight were so great he was gasping for air.

"Five hundred francs and a ticket are waiting for you in the office of Butz, the notary on the Bundesgasse," Barlach said calmly. "The trip will do you good. Paris is a beautiful city, the most beautiful one I know, apart from Constantinople; and the French—I don't know, Fortschig, I think the French are the best and most cultivated fellows around. Not even a dyed-in-the-wool Turk can compare with them."

"To Paris, to Paris," the poor devil stammered.

"But before you go, I will need your help with something that's eating me up," Barlach said, gazing sharply at the little man. "It's a terrible thing."

"A crime?" Fortschig was quaking.

"A crime that must be exposed."

Fortschig slowly put the "Little Rose" in the ashtray next to him. "Is it dangerous, what I have to do?" he asked softly, with wide-open eyes.

"No," the old man said. "It is not dangerous. And to remove even the remotest possibility of danger, I'm sending you to Paris. But you have to follow my instructions. When is the next issue of *Apfelschuss* due?"

"I don't know. Whenever I have some money."

"When can you send out an issue?" the inspector asked.

"Right away," Fortschig replied.

"Do you produce the *Apfelschuss* by yourself?" Barlach wanted to know.

"Alone. With a typewriter and an old duplicating machine," the editor replied.

"In how many copies?"

"Forty-five. It's a very small newspaper," Fortschig softly replied from his chair. "I've never had more than fifteen subscriptions."

The inspector reflected for a moment.

"The next issue of *Apfelschuss* has to come out in a huge edition. Three hundred copies. I'll pay. All I expect from you is that you write a certain article for this issue: the rest of the paper is all yours to fill any way you want to. This article" (he handed him the long sheet of paper) "will contain what I have written here: but in your language, Fortschig, I want you to write the way you did in your best times. You don't need to know any more than the information I'm giving you, not even the name of the doctor this diatribe is aimed at. Don't be irritated by my allegations: trust me, they are true, I can vouch for that. In the article, which you will send to certain hospitals, there will be only one lie, and that is that you, Fortschig, hold the proof of your assertions in your hands and know the name of the doctor. That's the dangerous part. And that is why you have to go to Paris as soon as you've brought the *Apfelschuss* to the post office. That same night."

"I will write, and I will go," the writer assured Barlach, holding the sheet of paper the old man had given him. He looked transformed. He was virtually skipping with joy.

"You will not tell anyone about your trip," Barlach commanded.

"No one will know it," Fortschig swore, "not a soul."

The old man wanted to know how much the issue would cost.

"Four hundred francs," the little man demanded with shining eyes, proud of his newly found affluence.

The inspector nodded. "You can pick up the money from my good old Butz. If you hurry, he'll give it to you today, I've already told him on the phone.—So you'll leave as soon as the issue is out?" he asked again, filled with an invincible mistrust.

"Immediately," Fortschig swore, holding up three fingers for emphasis. "That same night. For Paris."

But the old man was not reassured after Fortschig had left. The writer had struck him as more unreliable than ever. He wondered whether he shouldn't ask Lutz to have him guarded.

"Nonsense," he said then. "They dismissed me. I'll solve the Emmenberger case on my own. Fortschig will write the article against Emmenberger, and since he'll be leaving town, I won't have to lose any sleep over him. Not even Hungertobel needs to know anything about this. I wish he would come now. I could use a 'Little Rose.'"

Part Two

THE ABYSS

And so it came to pass that at nightfall on Friday—it was the last day of the year—the inspector, his legs propped up under blankets on the back seat of a car, reached the city of Zürich. Hungertobel himself sat at the wheel, and he was driving even more carefully than usual. He was worried about his friend. The city burst into glowing cascades of light. Hungertobel was caught in a dense swarm of cars that came gliding into this brilliance from all sides, slipping off into side streets and opening themselves, disgorging their contents, men, women, all greedy for this night, this end of the year, all ready to start a new one and go on living. The old man sat motionless in the back of the car, lost in the darkness of the small, arched space. He asked Hungertobel not to take the most direct route. With a lowering stare, he observed the tireless commotion. He was ordinarily not very fond of Zürich, four hundred thousand Swiss in one spot seemed a little excessive; he hated the Bahnhofstrasse they were driving along, but on this mysterious trip to an uncertain and menacing destination—(on this trip to reality, as he had said to Hungertobel)—the city fascinated him. From the black, lusterless sky a fine rain began to fall, then snow, then rain again, silver threads in the lights. People, people! Ever new mobs of them thronging both sides of the street behind curtains of snow and rain, ghostlike faces behind the windows of crowded trams flashing into view, hands clutching newspapers, fantastic forms in the silver light, passing, gone. For the first time since he had fallen ill, Barlach felt like a man whose time had passed, who had lost his battle with death, that irrevocable battle. The reason that irresistibly drew him to Zürich, this suspicion, elaborated with dogged energy and yet merely a figment dreamed up, by accident, on the tired waves of his illness, seemed futile and worthless now; why make the effort, to what end, for what purpose? He longed to sink back into an endless, dreamless sleep.

Hungertobel cursed inwardly, he felt the resignation of the old man behind him and reproached himself for not having put a stop to this adventure. The vague nocturnal surface of the lake flooded into view, the car glided slowly across the bridge. A traffic policeman appeared, an automaton with mechanically propelled arms and legs. Fleetingly Barlach thought of Fortschig (miserable Fortschig, who was now sitting in his dirty garret in Bern, feverishly writing the pamphlet), and then he lost this anchor, too. He leaned back and closed his eyes. The tiredness in him grew, a ghostly, towering thing.

"You'll die," he thought. "One day you'll die, within a year, just as cities, nations, and continents will die one day. You'll croak," he thought, "that's the word: croak—and the earth will still revolve around the sun, on the same imperceptibly wavering, stubborn, inexhorable course, racing and yet so calm, on and on, on and on. What does it matter whether this city here lives or whether that gray, watery, lifeless surface covers everything, the houses, the towers, the lights, the people—were those the leaden waves of the Dead Sea I saw through the darkness of rain and snow when we were crossing the bridge?"

He felt cold. The coldness of the universe, a fleeting breath of unimaginably vast and stony coldness, descended on him for a second, for an eternity.

He opened his eyes and stared out again. The theater building appeared and vanished. The old man saw his friend in the front of the car: the doctor's calm, kindly presence comforted him (he sensed nothing of Hungertobel's distress). Touched by the breath of the void, he become awake and courageous again. At the university they made a right turn, the road climbed, darkened, one curve succeeded another, the old man let himself drift, his senses keen, his mind sharply observant, imperturbable.

THE DWARF

Hungertobel's car stopped in a park whose firs imperceptibly blended with the forest. That at least was what Barlach presumed, for he could only guess at the edge of the forest that marked the horizon. Up here it was snowing in large pure flakes; through the falling snow the old man could obscurely make out the front of the long-stretched hospital building. The brightly lit entrance, near which the car stood, was deeply set into the facade and flanked by two windows behind artistically wrought gratings—well positioned to watch the entrance, the inspector thought. Hungertobel lit a "Little Rose," and without saying a word left the car and disappeared in the entrance. The old man was alone. He leaned forward and scanned the building, as far as that was possible in the dark. "Sonnenstein," he thought. "Reality." The snow fell more thickly, not a single one of the many windows was lighted, only once in a while a vague gleam flickered through the falling masses of snow; the white, modern steel and glass construction lay lifeless before him. The old man became restless, Hungertobel seemed in no hurry to come back; he looked at his watch and realized hardly a minute had passed. "I'm nervous," he thought, and leaned back with the intention of closing his eyes.

At that moment Barlach's glance fell through the broad runnels of melting snow on the car window and espied a figure hanging from the bars of the window to the left of the entrance. At first he thought he was seeing a monkey, but then he recognized with surprise that it was a dwarf, the kind that is sometimes used in a circus for the public's entertainment. The little hands and feet were naked and gripped the bars as a monkey's would, while the massive head was turned toward the inspector. It was a shriveled, ancient face of a bestial ugliness, with deep folds and crevices, degraded by nature herself, that gaped at the old man through large dark eyes, motionless, like a weather-worn, moss-covered stone. The inspector leaned forward and pressed his face against the wet window to see more clearly, but already the dwarf had vanished, with a cat-like leap backwards into the room, it seemed; the window was dark and empty. Now Hungertobel came, and behind him two nurses, doubly white in the incessant snowfall. The doctor opened the car door and was shocked when he saw Barlach's pale face.

"What's happening?" he whispered.

"Nothing," the old man replied. "I just have to get used to this modern building. Reality is always a little different from what you imagine."

Hungertobel sensed that the old man was hiding something and looked at him suspiciously. "Well," he replied, whispering as before, "this is it."

"Have you seen Emmenberger?" the inspector whispered.

"I talked to him," Hungertobel reported. "I have no doubt whatsoever, Hans, it's him. I wasn't mistaken in Ascona."

The two men fell silent. Outside, the nurses were waiting somewhat impatiently.

"We're chasing a phantom," Hungertobel thought to himself. "Emmenberger is a harmless doctor, and this hospital is like any other, just more expensive."

In the back of the car, in the now almost impenetrable shadow, sat the inspector, fully aware of what Hungertobel was thinking.

"When will he examine me?" he asked.

"Now," Hungertobel replied.

The doctor saw how the old man was regaining his verve. "Then say goodbye to me here, Samuel," Barlach said, "you're incapable of putting on an act, and no one must know that we're friends. A lot depends on this first interrogation."

"Interrogation?"

"What else?" was the inspector's wry response. "Emmenberger will examine me and I will interrogate him."

They shook hands.

The nurses came. Now there were four. The old man was lifted onto a gleaming metal stretcher. Sinking back, he saw Hungertobel handing out the suitcase. Then the old man looked up, into a black, empty plane from which the flakes descended in silent, incomprehensible whirls, dancing, floating, shining in the light before touching his face for a moment, wet and cold. "The snow won't stay on the ground," he thought. As the wheelchair was rolled through the entrance, he could hear Hungertobel's car leaving. "He's leaving, he's leaving," he said quietly to himself. Above him was a gleaming white, vaulted ceiling interrupted by wide strips of mirror-glass in which he saw himself stretched out and helpless; smoothly and noiselessly, the stretcher glided through mysterious corridors; not even the nurses' steps could be heard. Black numbers clung to the glittering whiteness right and left, the only mark distinguishing the doors from the walls. Now he was passing a niche; in the half-light inside it stood the naked firm body of a statue. Once again Barlach was received into the gentle yet cruel world of a hospital.

And behind him the red, fat face of the nurse who was pushing the stretcher.

The old man had again crossed his hands behind his neck.

"Is there a dwarf around here?" he asked in High German, for he had been registered as a Swiss living abroad.

The nurse laughed. "But Herr Kramer," she said, "What makes you think that?"

She spoke High German with a Swiss coloration, from which he concluded that she was from Bern. Her answer made him suspicious, but her accent struck him as a positive sign. At least he was among Bernese.

"What is your name, Nurse?"

"I am Nurse Kläri."

"From Bern, right?"

"Yes, from Biglen, Herr Kramer."

I'll work on her, the inspector thought.

THE INTERROGATION

The nurse rolled Barlach into a room that at first glance appeared to be made entirely of glaringly bright panes of glass. There he saw two figures: one of them slightly bent, gaunt, a man of the world even in his white lab coat, with heavy horn-rimmed glasses that could not quite conceal the scar over his right eyebrow: Dr. Fritz Emmenberger. The old man's glance merely brushed past the doctor at first; he paid more attention to the woman next to his suspect. Women made him curious. He looked at her distrustfully. Like most men of Bern, he found professional women uncanny. The woman was beautiful, he had to admit, and as an old bachelor he was doubly susceptible to that; she was a lady, he could tell that at first glance, the way she stood there, so elegant and so reserved in her white smock next to Emmenberger (who could, after all, be a mass murderer), but she seemed just a bit too noble for him. "You could put her right on a pedestal," the inspector thought bitterly.

"*Grüessech,*" he said, dropping the High German he had just been speaking with Nurse Kläri, "it's a pleasure to meet such a famous doctor."

"Why, you're speaking Bernese German," the doctor replied, also in dialect.

"I may live abroad, but that doesn't mean I can't still pronounce '*Miuchmauchterli,*'" the old man muttered.

"Well, you just proved it," Emmenberger laughed. "It takes a Bernese to pronounce '*Miuchmauchterli*' properly."

"Hungertobel is right," Barlach thought. "This is not Nehle. No Berliner could ever pronounce that word as he did."

He looked at the lady again.

"My assistant, Doctor Marlok," the doctor introduced her.

"Hm," said the old man dryly, "glad to meet you too." And then, abruptly, turning his head a little toward the doctor, he asked, "Weren't you in Germany once, Dr. Emmenberger?"

"Once, years ago," the doctor replied, "I was there, but mostly in Santiago de Chile." Nothing betrayed what he might be thinking, or whether the question had unsettled him.

"In Chile, in Chile," the old man said, and then again: "In Chile, in Chile."

Emmenberger lit a cigarette and went to the switchboard; now the room lay in semi-darkness, sparsely lit by a small blue lamp above the inspector. Only the operating table was visible, and the faces of the white figures standing before him; the old man also noticed that the room was closed off by a window through which a few distant lights cast their rays. The red tip of Emmenberger's cigarette moved up and down.

A thought suddenly struck the inspector: "There's usually no smoking in this sort of room. I've unsettled him already."

"Where's Hungertobel?" the doctor asked.

"I sent him away," Barlach answered. "I want you to examine me in his absence."

The doctor pushed up his glasses. "I think we may safely put our trust in Dr. Hungertobel."

"Certainly," Barlach replied.

"You are ill," Emmenberger continued, "the operation was dangerous and is not always successful. Hungertobel told me that you are aware of this. That is good. We doctors need courageous patients whom we can tell the truth. I would have welcomed Hungertobel's presence during the examination, and I am sorry that he acceded to your wish. As doctors, we should cooperate, science itself demands it."

"As a colleague, I can well understand that," the inspector replied.

"What do you mean?" Emmenberger asked. "You're not a doctor, as far as I know."

"Simple," the old man laughed. "You track down diseases, I ferret out war criminals."

Emmenberger lit another cigarette. "I guess that's not without its dangers, for a private citizen," he said nonchalantly.

"Exactly," Barlach replied. "And now, in the midst of my search, I get sick and come to you. That's what I call bad luck, getting shipped to the Sonnenstein clinic; or is it good luck?"

"I cannot give a prognosis yet," Emmenberger replied. "Hungertobel wasn't exactly optimistic."

"Well, you haven't examined me yet," said the old man. "and that's the reason why I didn't want good old Hungertobel present. We have to be openminded if we want to make headway in our case. And I think that both you and I want to make headway. There is nothing worse than forming an opinion, about a criminal or a sickness, before one has studied the suspect in his environment and examined his habits."

"That's true," the doctor replied. "As a doctor I don't know anything about criminology, but what you say makes sense. Well, Herr Kramer, I hope that here you'll be able to recover somewhat from the rigors of your profession."

Then he lit a third cigarette and said, "I think the war criminals will leave you in peace here."

Emmenberger's answer made the old man suspicious for a moment. "Who is interrogating whom?" he thought, looking into Emmenberger's face, a mask-like visage in the light of the single lamp, the eyes behind the gleaming spectacles abnormally large and, it seemed, glittering with mockery.

"Dear doctor," he said, "surely you wouldn't claim that in a certain country there is no such thing as cancer."

"Surely you're not implying that there are war criminals in Switzerland!" Emmenberger laughed.

The old man scrutinized the doctor. "What happened in Germany happens in every country, given certain conditions. The conditions may vary. No man, no nation is an exception. I have been told by a Jew, Dr. Emmenberger, a man who underwent an operation without anesthesia in a concentration camp, that there is only one difference between human beings: the difference between the tormentors and the tormented. But I believe there is also the difference between the tempted and the spared. That puts you and me, as Swiss citizens, among those who were spared the ordeal of temptation, which is a blessing and not a fault, as many say; for we are supposed to pray: 'Lead us not into temptation.' So I have come to Switzerland, not to look for war criminals in general, but to ferret out *one particular* war criminal, although I have little more than an unclear picture of him. But now I am sick, Dr. Emmenberger, the hunt has collapsed overnight, and the quarry does not even know how close I was on his traces. A pathetic spectacle."

"In that case your chances of finding your man are very slim," the doctor replied indifferently, exhaling a puff of smoke that formed a milky, luminous ring above the old man's head. Barlach saw him giving a sign to the woman with his eyes. She handed him a syringe. Emmenberger vanished for a moment into the darkness of the room. When he reappeared, he was holding a vial.

"Your chances are slim," he said again as he filled the syringe with a colorless liquid.

But the inspector contradicted him.

"I still have a weapon," he said. "Let's take your method, doctor. I come to your hospital all the way from Bern through snow and sleet on this last dreary day of the year, and you receive me in the operating room for my first examination. Why do you do this? It's unusual, wouldn't you say, for a patient to be shoved straightaway into a room that would frighten him? You do this because you want to fill me with fear, for you can only be my doctor if you dominate me, and I am a noncompliant patient, I'm sure Hungertobel told you that. So you decided to give this demonstration. You want to dominate me in order to cure me, and fear is one of the means you are obliged to employ. It's the same in my fiendish profession. Our methods are the same. My only leverage against the man I am looking for is fear."

The needle in Emmenberger's hand was pointed at the old man. "You're a shrewd psychologist," the doctor laughed. "It's true, I wanted to impress you a bit with this room. Fear is a necessary tool. But before I exercise *my* art, let's hear the rest about yours. How will you proceed? I'm curious. The hunted man does not know you're hunting him, at least those are your own words."

"He senses it without being sure, and that's more dangerous for him," Barlach replied. "He knows that I'm in Switzerland and that I'm looking for a war criminal. He'll silence his suspicion and assure himself over and over that I'm looking for someone else and not him. Because, you see, he escaped from the world of unlimited crime into Switzerland, and by a masterly trick he left himself behind. A great secret. But in the darkest chamber of his heart he will know that I'm looking for *him* and not for anyone else, him and always and only him. And he will be afraid, and the more unlikely he thinks it is that I am really looking for him, the more his fear will grow, while I, Doctor, lie in my bed in this hospital with my sickness, with my impotence." He stopped talking.

Emmenberger looked at him strangely, almost with pity, still holding the syringe.

"I doubt that you will succeed," he said calmly. "But I wish you luck."

The old man did not move a muscle. "He will die of fear," he said.

Emmenberger slowly laid the syringe on the little glass and metal table that stood next to the stretcher. There it lay, a malignant sharp thing. Emmenberger stood slightly bent forward. "Do you think so? he finally said. "Do you really think so?" His narrow eyes contracted almost imperceptibly behind his glasses. "It's amazing to find someone still as hopeful as you are, and as optimistic, in these times. Your way of thinking is bold; let's hope you don't find yourself duped by reality one of these days. It would be too bad if you came to disheartening results." He said this softly, slightly bemused. Then he slowly walked back into the darkness of the room, and the lights went on with a blinding glare. Emmenberger stood by the switchboard.

"I will examine you later, Herr Kramer," he said, smiling. "Your illness is serious. You know that. It could be fatal—that suspicion has not been cancelled. That, unfortunately, is my impression after our conversation. You have been open with me, I owe you the same. The examination will not be easy, it requires a bit of surgery. But we'd rather have that after the New Year, don't you agree? Why disrupt a nice holiday? The main thing is that I have you under my wing."

Barlach did not reply.

Emmenberger extinguished the cigarette. "Good Lord, Doctor Marlok," he said, "I've been smoking in the operation room. Herr Kramer is an exciting visitor. You should slap his wrist and mine."

"What's this?" asked the old man when Dr. Marlok handed him two reddish pills.

"Just a sedative," she said. But he drank the water she gave him with even greater uneasiness.

"Call for the nurse," Emmenberger ordered from the switchboard.

Nurse Kläri appeared at the door. To the inspector, she looked like a good-natured executioner. "Hangmen are always good-natured," he thought.

"Which room did you prepare for our Herr Kramer?" asked Dr. Emmenberger.

"Number seventy-two, Doctor," Nurse Kläri replied.

"Let's give him room number fifteen," said Emmenberger, "we'll have better control over him there."

The inspector was again overcome by the tiredness he had felt in Hungertobel's car.

When the nurse rolled the old man back into the hallway, the stretcher made a sharp turn, and Barlach, tearing himself out of his drowsiness, saw Emmenberger's face.

He saw that the doctor was observing him carefully, smiling and serene.

Gripped by a fit of feverish shivering, he fell back.

THE ROOM

When he awoke (it was still night, close to ten thirty; he must have slept about three hours, he thought), he was in another room, which he surveyed with surprise and not without apprehension, but still with a certain satisfaction: for he hated hospital rooms, and it pleased him that this room was more like a studio, a technical room, cold and impersonal, as far as he could tell in the blue light of the night lamp that had been left burning on his left. The bed in which he was lying—dressed in a night-shirt and well covered—was still the same stretcher on which he had been brought in; he recognized it right away, though it had been converted with a few simple manual adjustments. "They're practical here," the old man said quietly into the stillness. He swiveled the head of the lamp, sweeping the room with its beam; a curtain appeared, presumably there was a window behind it; the cloth was embroidered with strange plants and animals that gleamed in the light. "You can tell I'm hunting," he said to himself.

He settled back in his pillow and reviewed what he had accomplished. It was little enough. He had carried out his plan. Now it was necessary to weave the net further, spin the threads tighter. It was necessary to act. But how, and how to begin? He did not know. He pressed a button on the little table. Nurse Kläri appeared.

"Well, well, our nurse from Biglen by the Burgdorf-Thun railroad line," the old man greeted her. "You see how well I know Switzerland, even though I've lived abroad all these years."

"Well, Herr Kramer, what is it? You finally woke up?" she said, with her round fists on her hips.

The old man looked at his watch again. "It's only ten thirty."

"Are you hungry?" she asked.

"No," said the inspector, who felt weak.

"You see, the gentleman's not even hungry. I'll call Doctor Marlok, you've met her. She'll give you another injection," the nurse retorted.

"Nonsense," the old man grumbled, "I wasn't given an injection. Why don't you switch on the ceiling lamp instead, I'd like to have a look at this room. One does like to know where one is."

He was quite angry.

A white, but not glaring, light went on. It was difficult to tell where it came from. Now the room was clearly visible. The ceiling above the old man—he noted this only now—was a single mirror. This annoyed him considerably: to see himself looming overhead might prove to be a bit eery. "Everywhere these mirrored ceilings," he thought, "it could drive you crazy." But secretly he was horrified by the skeleton staring down at him when he looked up. "This mirror is lying," he thought. "There are mirrors that distort everything, I can't be that emaciated." He looked around the room, forgetting the nurse, who was waiting without moving. On his left was a glass panel set in a gray surface into which naked figures were carved, dancing men and women, purely linear and yet three-dimensional; and from the right, greenish-gray wall, between door and curtain, tilting into the room like the lid of a grand piano, hung Rembrandt's "Anatomy," a seemingly senseless detail, but it was calculated to combine with the dancers in a way that gave the room a frivolous air; and this impression was only increased by the black, rough-hewn wooden cross that hung over the door in which the nurse stood.

"Well, now, Nurse," he said, still amazed that the room had changed so much with the light; for before, he had only noticed the curtain and had seen nothing of the dancing men and women, the

"Anatomy," and the cross; and now the sight of this unknown world filled him with apprehension: "Well, now, Nurse, this is a rather peculiar room for a hospital that is supposed to make people healthy and not insane."

"We're on Mount Sonnenstein," Nurse Kläri replied, folding her hands over her belly. "We try to meet all requests," she chattered, shining with probity, "the most pious ones and the others too. My word of honor, if you don't care for the 'Anatomy,' you can have Botticelli's 'Birth of Venus' or a Picasso."

"In that case I'd rather have 'Knight, Death, and Devil,'" the inspector said.

Nurse Kläri pulled out a notebook. "Knight, Death, and Devil," she said as she wrote the words down. "We'll put it up tomorrow. A lovely picture for a death-room. Congratulations. The gentleman has good taste."

"I think," replied the old man, amazed at the crudeness of this Nurse Kläri, "I think I'm not quite at that point yet."

Nurse Kläri pensively wagged her red, fleshy head. "Oh yes, you are," she said emphatically. "This place is for dying only. Exclusively. I have never seen anyone leave Ward Three. And you *are* in Ward Three, that's all there is to it. Everyone has to die some time. Read what I have written about it. It was published by the Liechti printshop in Walkringen."

The nurse pulled a little pamphlet out of her bosom and put it on the old man's bed: *Kläri Glauber: Death, the Goal and Purpose of our Life on Earth. A practical guide.*

"Shall I fetch Doctor Marlok?" she asked triumphantly.

"No," the inspector replied, still holding the goal and purpose of our life in his hands. "I don't need her. But I would like the curtain over to the side. And the window open."

The curtain was pulled to the side; the light went out. The old man turned off the night lamp.

Nurse Kläri's massive figure disappeared in the door's illuminated rectangle, but before it closed, he asked:

"Nurse, one more time! You answer all questions straight off the cuff, I'm sure you can give me the truth about this: Is there a dwarf in this house?"

"Of course," came the brutal reply from the rectangle. "You saw him."

Then the door closed.

"Nonsense," he thought. "I will leave Ward Three. What's there to stop me? I'll call Hungertobel. I'm too sick to do anything worthwhile against Emmenberger. Tomorrow I'm going back to Salem hospital."

He was afraid and was not ashamed to admit it.

Outside was the night and around him the darkness of the room. The old man lay on his bed, hardly breathing.

"At some point the bells should ring," he thought. "The bells of Zürich, ringing in the new year."

Somewhere a clock struck twelve.

The old man waited.

Again a clock struck somewhere, and then again, each time twelve merciless strokes. Stroke after stroke, like the strokes of a hammer on a bronze gate.

No ringing of bells, not even the faintest sound of a happy, jubilant crowd.

The new year came silently.

"The world is dead," the inspector thought over and over: "The world is dead. The world is dead."

He felt a cold sweat on his forehead, drops slowly gliding along his temple. His eyes were wide open. He lay motionless. Humble.

Once again he heard twelve distant strokes, dying away over a desolate city. Then he felt himself sinking into some shoreless ocean, some dark and vast space.

He woke up at dawn, in the twilight of the new day.

"They didn't ring in the new year," he thought again and again.

The room felt more menacing than ever.

For a long time he stared into the rising dawn, the gradually brightening green-gray shadows, until he realized:

The window was barred.

DOCTOR MARLOK

"I see we've woken up," said a voice from the door to the inspector, who was staring at the barred window. Into the room, which was filling more and more with a foggy, phantom-like morning light, stepped an old woman in a doctor's white coat. In her withered, swollen features Barlach recognized with difficulty and with horror the face of the doctor he had seen with Emmenberger in the operation room. He stared at her, tired and shaken by disgust. Without paying any attention to the inspector, she raised her skirt and injected a syringe through her stocking into her thigh; then she stood up straight, pulled out a pocket mirror, and applied make-up. The old man watched this procedure with fascination. He seemed no longer to exist for the woman. Her features lost their coarseness and regained the freshness and clarity he had noticed, so that, leaning motionless against the door jamb, the woman standing in his room was the one whose beauty had struck him at the time of his arrival.

"I understand," said the old man, slowly awakening from his torpor, but still exhausted and confused. "Morphine."

"Certainly," she said. "It's a necessity in this world—Inspector Barlach."

The old man stared out into the morning, which was darkening; for it was raining outside, pouring into the snow that, he presumed, was still on the ground, and then he said softly, and as if in passing:

"You know who I am."

Then he stared out the window again.

"We know who you are," the doctor confirmed, still leaning against the door, both hands buried in the pockets of her smock.

"How did you find out?" he asked, though in fact he was not at all curious.

She tossed a newspaper on his bed.

It was the *Bund*.

On the front page was his picture, as the old man noticed right away, a snapshot taken in the spring, when he had still smoked Ormond-Brazils, and the caption said: "Retired: Hans Barlach, Detective Inspector of the Bern City Police."

"Of course," the inspector muttered.

And then, as he cast a second, disconcerted and irritated glance at the newspaper, he saw the date.

It was the first time he lost his composure.

"The date," he shouted hoarsely: "The date, Doctor! The date of the newspaper!"

"So?" she asked, not a flicker of movement in her face.

"It's the fifth of January," the inspector gasped desperately. Now he understood the absence of the New Year's bells, the whole horror of the past night.

"Did you expect a different date?" she asked sarcastically, and with obvious curiosity, raising her eyebrows slightly.

He screamed: "What did you do to me?" and tried to sit up, but fell back into the bed.

His arms waved about in the air a few times, then he lay motionless again.

The doctor pulled out a cigarette case and took out a cigarette.

She seemed untouched by anything.

"I don't want any smoking in my room," said Barlach, quietly but firmly.

"The window is barred," the doctor replied, with a nod toward the raindrops running down behind the iron bars.

"I don't think you have any say around here."

Then she turned to the old man and stepped up to his bed, her hands buried in the pockets of her coat.

"Insulin," she said, looking down at him. "The boss gave you an insulin treatment. His specialty." She laughed. "Do you intend to arrest the man?"

"Emmenberger operated without anesthesia on a German doctor named Nehle and murdered him," was Barlach's cold-blooded reply. He sensed that he had to win this woman over.

He was determined to risk everything.

"He did a lot more than that, our doctor," she replied.

"You know it!"

"Certainly."

"You admit that Emmenberger was the camp doctor in Stutthof under the name of Nehle?" he asked feverishly.

"Of course."

"You admit the murder of Nehle also?"

"Why not?"

With one stroke Barlach found his suspicion confirmed—this monstrous, abstruse suspicion, which had begun as a hunch when Hungertobel turned pale at the sight of an old photograph, and which he had been carrying through these endless days like a gigantic load. Exhausted, he looked out the window. One by one, drops of water were running down the bars, catching the light with a silvery gleam. He had longed for this moment of knowledge as for a moment of rest.

"If you know everything," he said, "you are guilty too."

His voice sounded tired and sad.

The doctor gazed down at him with such a peculiar look that her silence unsettled him. She pushed up her right sleeve. On her lower arm, burned deeply into the flesh, was a number, like a cattle brand. "Do I have to show you my back too?" she asked.

"You were in the concentration camp?" the inspector exclaimed, staring at her in dismay and raising himself slightly, with a great effort, using his right arm for support.

"Edith Marlok, inmate 4466 in death camp Stutthof near Danzig." Her voice was cold and dead.

The old man fell back into his pillow. He cursed his sickness, his weakness, his helplessness.

"I was a communist," she said, pushing down the sleeve.

"And how did you manage to survive the camp?"

"That's simple," she replied, and she took in his gaze with complete indifference, as if nothing could move her any longer, no human feeling and not even the most terrible fate:

"I became Emmenberger's lover."

"But that's impossible!" the inspector exclaimed.

She looked at him with surprise.

"A torturer had mercy on a sick and starving dog," she finally said. "Becoming the lover of an SS doctor was an extremely rare opportunity for a woman in Stutthof. Any way to save yourself is good. You yourself are trying everything to get out of Sonnenstein."

Feverish and shaking, he tried for a third time to sit up.

"Are you still his lover?"

"Of course. Why not?"

"You can't do that!" he shouted. "Emmenberger is a monster! You were a communist, you're not without convictions!"

"Yes, I had convictions," she said calmly. "I was convinced that this sad thing of stone and mud that revolves around the sun deserves to be loved, that it is our duty to help humanity, in the name of reason, to get rid of poverty and exploitation. That was my faith, and it wasn't just a slogan. And when the postcard painter with the ridiculous moustache and the kitshy strand of hair on his forehead seized power—that's the technical term for the crime he committed from then on—I fled to the land in which, like all communists, I believed; to the mother of all virtue, the venerable Soviet Union. Oh, I had my convictions, and staked them against the world. I was as determined as you are, Inspector, to fight against evil until the blessed end of my life."

"We must not give up this struggle," Barlach replied softly. He had sunk back into his pillows and was shivering with cold.

"May I request that you look in the mirror above you," she said.

"I've already seen myself," he replied, anxiously avoiding an upward glance.

She laughed. "A lovely skeleton grinning down at you there, representing the chief detective of the city of Bern! Our doctrine of the necessity of fighting against evil, and of not giving up under any conditions, holds true in a vacuum or, what amounts to the same thing, on a desk; but not on this planet on which we fly through the universe like witches on a broom. My faith was great, so great that I did not despair when I felt all around me the misery of the Russian masses, the anguish of this mighty land, which would not be ennobled by any violence, but only by freedom of the spirit. When the Russians buried me in their prisons and shoved me, without a trial and without a sentence, from one camp to another, without my knowing why, I never doubted that this too had a meaning in the great plan of history. When that marvelous pact came about, the one between Mr. Stalin and Mr. Hitler, I recognized the need for it. After all, the great Communist fatherland had to be saved. But one morning, deep in the winter of nineteen-forty, after several weeks of traveling westward in a cattle car from Siberia, Russian soldiers chased me and a crowd of ragged specters across a miserable wooden bridge. Beneath us a river, dirty, sluggish, dragging along clumps of ice and wood. And when, on the other shore, the black shapes of the SS emerged from the morning mist to receive us, I realized the betrayal, not only of us poor godforsaken devils who were now tottering toward Stutthof, but of the idea of Communism itself, which has no meaning unless it is identical with the idea of charity and love of humanity. But now I have crossed the bridge, Inspector, I have crossed those black, swaying planks forever, and beneath them the river Bug—that's the name of that Tartarus. Now I know the stuff that human beings are made of. You can do anything with them, whatever some tyrant or an Emmenberger might think of for his entertainment or to test his theories. I know that any confession can be forced from the mouth of a human being, because human will is limited, but the number of tortures is legion. Abandon hope, all ye who enter here! I abandoned hope. It's nonsense to resist and fight for a better world. Man himself desires his hell, prepares it in his thoughts, and brings it about with his deeds. Everywhere the same thing, in Stutthof and here in Sonnenstein, everywhere the same gruesome melody, the same sinister chords rising up from the abyss of the human soul. If the camp near Danzig was the hell of the Jews, the Christians, and the Communists, this hospital here, in the middle of dear old Zürich, is the hell of the rich."

"What do you mean by that? Those are strange words you are using," said the old man, staring at the doctor, who fascinated him as much as she frightened him.

"You are curious," she said, "and you seem to be proud of it. You've crawled into the fox's den, and there's no way out. Don't count on me. Human beings mean nothing to me, not even Emmenberger, who is my lover."

THE HELL OF THE RICH

"Why for this lost world's sake, Inspector," she began talking again, "why were you not content with your daily larcenies, and why did you have to nose your way in here, where you don't belong? But I guess a retired police dog yearns for higher things."

The doctor laughed.

"The place to look for injustice is where you can find it," the old man replied. "The law is the law."

"I see, you like mathematics," she replied, and lit another cigarette. She still stood by his bed, not with the hesitant and careful air of a doctor approaching a sickbed, but the way one might stand next to a criminal who is already strapped to a gurney and whose execution one has recognized as correct and desirable, a rational procedure to extinguish a useless existence. "I thought right away you're the type of fool who swears by mathematics. The law is the law. $X = X$. The most monstrous phrase ever to rise to the eternally bloody night sky that hangs above us," she laughed. "As if there were some sort of moral law that held true for man regardless of the amount of power he possesses. The law is not the law. Power is the law; that is the decree written over the valleys of our destruction. Nothing is itself in this world, everything is a lie. When we say law, we mean power; when we pronounce the word 'power,' we think of wealth, and when the word 'wealth' passes our lips, we hope to enjoy the vices of the world. The law is vice, the law is wealth, the law is cannons, monopolies, political parties. Whatever we say, it is never illogical, except for the statement that the law is the law, which is the only lie. Mathematics lies, reason, intelligence, art, they all lie. What do you want, Inspector? We're deposited on some brittle shoal, without being asked, and without knowing why; there we sit staring into a universe, monstrously empty and monstrously full, a meaningless waste, drifting toward those distant cataracts that we'll eventually reach—the only thing we know. We live in order to die, we breathe and speak, we love, we have children and grandchildren, so that we and our loved ones and those we have brought forth out of our own flesh can end up as carrion and disintegrate into the indifferent, dead elements we are composed of. The cards were shuffled and dealt and gathered together: *c'est ça*. And because all we have is this drifting shoal of dirt and ice to which we cling, our dearest wish is that this our only life—this fleeting moment within view of the rainbow that arches across the foam and steam of the abyss—should be a happy one; that the earth—our only, meager grace—should give us all her abundance for the brief time she carries us. But that is not how it is, and it never will be, and the crime, Inspector, is not that life isn't that way, that there is poverty and misery, it's that there are poor *and* rich people, that the ship in which we are all sinking together has cabins for the rich and powerful next to the mass quarters for the poor. We all have to die, they say, so it doesn't matter. To die is to die. Oh this farcical mathematics! The dying of the poor is one thing, and the dying of the rich and powerful is another, and there is a world in between, the stage on which the bloody tragicomedy between the weak and the powerful takes place. The poor man dies the way he lived, on a sack in a cellar, on a tattered mattress if he climbs a little higher, or on the bloody field of honor if he reaches the top; but the rich man dies differently. He has lived in luxury and wants to die in luxury, he is cultivated and claps his hands as he kicks the bucket: Applause, my friends, the show is over! Life was a pose, dying an empty phrase, the funeral an advertisement, and the whole thing a good deal. *C'est ça.* If I could show you through this hospital, Inspector, through this Sonnenstein that has turned me into what I am now, neither a woman nor a man, just flesh that needs bigger and bigger amounts of morphine to make the kind of jokes about this world that it deserves—if I could, I would show you, a retired, used-up police dog, *how* the rich die. I would unlock the fantastic sickrooms for you where they're rotting, the rooms with the vulgar, sentimental décor and others, more subtly designed, those glittering cells of lust and torment, caprice and crime."

Barlach did not answer. He lay there, sick and motionless, his face turned away.

The doctor bent over him.

"I would tell you the names," she continued relentlessly, "of those who have died and are dying here, the names of the politicians, the bankers, the industrialists, the mistresses, and the widows, celebrities all of them, and those unknown crooks who have raked in millions at our expense and at no cost to themselves. So here's where they die, in this hospital. Some of them make blasphemous jokes about their own decrepitude, others revolt and spit out wild curses against their fate, against the fact that they own everything and yet have to die, and still others whine the most revolting prayers in their rooms full of silk and brocade, begging to be spared the substitution of paradise for the bliss of living down here. Emmenberger grants them everything, and they are insatiable, they gobble up everything he gives them; but they need more, they need hope: and this, too, he grants them. But the trust they give him is trust in the devil, and the hope he gives them is hell. They have forsaken God and found a new god. Voluntarily these sick people submit themselves to this marvelous doctor's tortures, just so they can live a few more days, a few more minutes (they hope), and postpone their separation from what they love more than heaven and hell, more than bliss and damnation: their power, and the earth that lent them that power. Here, too, the boss operates without anesthesia. Everything Emmenberger did in Stutthof, in that gray, convoluted city of barracks on the plain outside Danzig, he does here as well, in the middle of Switzerland, in the middle of Zürich, untouched by the police, by the laws of this land, and he does it in the name of science and humanity. Unwaveringly he gives these people what they want from him: tortures, nothing but tortures."

"No!" Barlach screamed. "No! He must be destroyed!"

"Then you'll have to destroy the human race," she replied.

Again he screamed his hoarse, desperate *No* and, with a great effort, raised himself up to a sitting position.

"No, no!" The words escaped his mouth, but they were merely whispers.

Casually, the doctor tapped his right shoulder, and he fell back onto his pillow.

"No, no," he gasped.

"You fool!" the doctor laughed. "What do you think this 'No, No!' will accomplish? In the black coal-district where I come from, I too said 'No, No' to this world full of misery and exploitation, and I started to work: in the Party, in evening courses, later at the University, and with more and more determination in the Party. I studied and worked for the sake of my No, No; but now, Inspector, standing before you in this white coat on this misty morning full of snow and rain, now I know that this No, No has become senseless, for the earth is too old to become a Yes, Yes, the embrace between Good and Evil was too intimate on the night of that godforsaken wedding between heaven and hell that gave birth to *this* humanity, they are too intertwined to ever be separated again, to allow anyone to say: This is well done and this is bad, this leads to the Good and this leads to Evil. Too late! We can no longer know what we do, what actions will result from our obedience or our revolt, what exploitation, what sticky residue of crime clings to the fruit we eat, to the bread and milk we give our children. We kill without seeing our victim or knowing about him, and we are killed without the murderer's knowledge. Too late! The temptation of this existence was too great and man was too small for the grace that consists of living and not being nothing instead. Now we are sick unto death, eaten by the cancer of our deeds. The world is rotten, Inspector, it's decaying like a badly stored fruit. What more do we want! The earth can no longer be made into a paradise, the infernal stream of lava we conjured up in the blasphemous days of our victories, our fame, and our wealth, and that now lights our night, can no longer be banished back into the caverns from which it arose. Only in our dreams can we win back what we have lost, in the radiant images of longing that can be attained with morphine. Thus I, Edith Marlok, a thirty-four-year-old woman, commit the crimes that are demanded of me in exchange for a colorless liquid which, injected beneath my skin, gives me the courage of contempt during the day and the beauty of dreams at night, a fleeting illusion of being in possession of what no longer exists: this world as God created it. *C'est ça.* Emmenberger, your compatriot, this son of the city of Bern, knows people and knows the uses to which they can be put. He applies his merciless levers where we are weakest: in the deadly consciousness of our eternal perdition."

"Go now," he whispered, "go now!"

The doctor laughed. Then she stood up, beautiful, proud, unapproachable.

"You want to fight Evil and are afraid of my *C'est ça,*" she said, putting on make-up again, leaning on the door. Above her, alone and meaningless, hung the old wooden cross. "You're already shuddering before a lowly servant of this world, who has been defiled and degraded a thousand times. How will you stand up to him, the Prince of Hell himself, Emmenberger?"

And then she tossed a second newspaper and a brown envelope on the old man's bed.

"Read your mail, sir. I think you'll be surprised at what you've accomplished with your good will!"

KNIGHT, DEATH, AND DEVIL

After the doctor had left the old man, he lay motionless for a long time. His suspicion had been confirmed, but what should have given him satisfaction filled him with horror. He had calculated correctly but sensed that he had made the wrong move. He was all too conscious of his body's helplessness. He had lost six days, six terrible days erased from his memory. Emmenberger knew who was after him, and had delivered his blow.

Then, finally, when Nurse Kläri came, he let her help him into a sitting position. Suspicious but defiant, determined to conquer his weakness and attack, he drank the coffee and ate the rolls she had brought.

"Nurse Kläri," he said, "I'm from the police, maybe it's better if we don't mince words."

"I know, Inspector Barlach," the nurse replied, a formidable menacing figure next to his bed.

"You know my name, so you're well informed," Barlach continued, taken aback. "Does that mean you know why I'm here?"

"You want to arrest our boss," she said, looking down at the old man.

"That's right, the boss," the inspector nodded. "And I imagine you know that your boss killed many people in the concentration camp at Stuttthof in Germany?"

"My boss has been converted," Nurse Kläri Glauber from Biglen proudly replied. "His sins have been forgiven."

"How come?" Barlach asked, astonished, staring at this monster of rectitude that stood by his bed, her hands folded over her belly, beaming and convinced.

"He read my brochure," said the nurse.

"The Goal and Purpose of Our Life on Earth?"

"That's right."

"This is nonsense!" the sick man cried angrily. "Emmenberger is still killing people."

"He used to kill out of hatred," the nurse cheerfully replied, "but now he kills out of love. He kills as a doctor, because man secretly longs for death. Just read my brochure. Man has to pass through death to his higher possibility."

"Emmenberger is a criminal," the inspector gasped, powerless against such sanctimony. She's a typical Emmenthal sectarian, he thought desperately, damn the lot of them.

"The meaning and purpose of our life on earth cannot be a crime," said Nurse Kläri, shaking her head disapprovingly as she cleared away the dishes.

"I will turn you over to the police as an accomplice," the inspector threatened, well aware that he was reaching for his cheapest weapon.

"You're on Ward Three," said Nurse Kläri Glauber, saddened by her patient's stubbornness, and left the room.

Angrily the old man reached for his mail. He recognized the envelope, it was the one Fortschig used to mail out his *Apfelschuss*. He opened it, and the newspaper fell out. It was written, as it had been for the past twenty-five years, on a rickety and by now no doubt rusty typewriter with a faulty *l* and *r*. "*Der Apfelschuss*. Swiss Protest Paper for the Inland and Surroundings. Published by Ulrich Friedrich Fortschig" was the printed title, and underneath, in typescript:

AN SS TORTURER AS
MEDICAL DIRECTOR

If I did not have the evidence (wrote Fortschig)—proofs of such terrible clarity and irrefutable logic that no criminological or poetic fancy could have produced them but only reality itself—I would be forced to dismiss as the spawn of a sick imagination the truth that compels me to write down what I know. Let Truth take the stand, then, even if it makes us turn pale, even if it forever unsettles the trust we still place—despite everything—in humanity. That a human being, a Bernese, went about his bloody trade under an assumed name in an extermination camp near Danzig—I dare not describe in detail with what bestiality—appalls us; but that he should be permitted to direct a clinic in Switzerland is a disgrace for which we can find no words, and an indication that these may very well be our own latter days. May these words, therefore, initiate a trial that, although terrible and embarrassing for our country, must be risked. For our reputation is at stake, the harmless rumor that we are still honestly muddling through the sinister jungles of these times—(perhaps earning a little more money than usual with watches, cheese, and some weapons of not very great significance). So I am taking action. We shall lose everything if we gamble with justice, which is not a plaything, even if it should prove embarrassing for us Pestalozzis to receive a rap on the knuckles. As for the criminal, a doctor in Zürich, whom we shall not pardon, as he did not pardon, whom we are extorting, as he extorted, and whom we shall finally murder, as he murdered countless people—we know it is a death sentence we are writing (Barlach read that line twice); of this director of a private clinic we demand—to put it plainly—that he turn himself in to the Zürich police. Mankind, which is capable of everything and is increasingly adept at murder far and beyond any other skill or proficiency, this mankind of which we in Switzerland are also a part—since we too bear within us the seeds of that unfortunate tendency to regard morality as unprofitable and to equate profit with morality—should finally learn by the example of this mass murderer, this beast felled by the bare force of words, that the despised spirit of Man will break open even the mouths of the silent and force them to utter their own destruction.

As much as this bombastic text complied with Barlach's original plan, which had simply and straightforwardly aimed at intimidating Emmenberger—the rest would somehow fall into place, he had thought with the careless self-confidence of an old criminologist— he now realized how thoroughly he had been mistaken. The doctor was not the type to be intimidated, far from it. Fortschig's life was in danger, the inspector felt, but he hoped that the writer was already in Paris and therefore safe.

And then it seemed that an unexpected possibility was presenting itself for Barlach to make contact with the outside world.

A worker stepped into the room with an enlarged reproduction of Dürer's "Knight, Death, and Devil" under his arm. The old man looked at him carefully. He was a goodnatured, somewhat seedy fellow in his late forties, wearing blue work clothes. He immediately started disassembling the "Anatomy."

"Hey!" said the inspector. "Come here."

The man kept working. From time to time he would drop a pair of pliers, or a screwdriver, and bend down awkwardly to pick them up.

"Hey, you!" Barlach called impatiently, since the worker paid him no attention. "I'm Police Inspector Barlach. Do you understand: my life is in danger. Leave this house after you have finished your work and go to Inspector Stutz, any child knows him around here. Or go to any police station and have them connect you with Stutz. Do you understand? I need this man. Tell him to come and see me."

The worker still paid no heed to the old man, who was straining in his bed to formulate the words. It was getting more and more difficult for him to speak. Having unscrewed the "Anatomy," the worker went on to examine the Dürer, first from close up and then holding it away from himself with both arms, arching his back. A milky light was falling through the window. For a moment it seemed to the old man that he could see a dim ball swimming behind white strips of fog. The worker's hair and moustache lit up. It had stopped raining outside. The worker shook his head several times; apparently he found the picture uncanny. He briefly turned to Barlach and said very slowly, shaking his head to and fro and enunciating each syllable with peculiar, exaggerated clarity:

"There is no devil."

"Yes, there is!" Barlach shouted hoarsely: "There is a devil, man! Right here in this hospital. Listen to me! I'm sure you've been told I'm crazy and nothing I say makes sense, but I'm telling you, my life is in danger, do you understand, my life is in danger: that is the truth, man, the truth, nothing but the truth!"

The worker had tightened the last screw on the picture and turned to Barlach, pointing with a grin at the knight who sat so motionless on his horse. He made some inarticulate, gurgling sounds that Barlach did not understand right away, but finally he could make out their meaning:

"Knight's a goner," said the man in the blue work clothes, pressing the words out of his obliquely twisted mouth: "Knight's a goner, knight's a goner!"

Not until the worker had left the room and clumsily slammed the door behind him did the old man realize that he had been talking to a deaf mute.

He reached for the second newspaper Dr. Marlok had given him, and opened it. It was the *Bernisches Bundesblatt*, devoted to news of the city of Bern.

Fortschig's face was the first thing he saw. Under the photograph were the words "Ulrich Friedrich Fortschig," and next to it: a cross.

FORTSCHIG†

"The wretched life of one of our city's more notorious than famous writers ended on Tuesday night. The cause of his death has not yet been determined." As Barlach read these words, he felt as if he was being choked. "This man," continued the *Bernisches Bundesblatt*'s reporter in his characteristically unctuous manner, "whom Nature endowed with such beautiful gifts, did not know how to properly steward his talents. He began with expressionistic plays that produced a stir among the boulevard literati, but increasingly lost the ability to give shape to his imaginative powers" (at least they were imaginative powers, was the old man's bitter response), "until he hit upon the unfortunate idea of issuing his own newspaper, the *Apfelschuss,* which he proceeded to issue irregularly enough in an edition of approximately fifty typewritten copies. Anyone who has read the contents of this scandal sheet knows enough: it consisted of attacks, not only against everything we hold sacred but against well known and respected personalities as well. He deteriorated steadily, and was often seen drunk, sporting the famous yellow scarf that earned him the nickname 'lemon' in many parts of the city, staggering from one pub to another, accompanied by a few students who cheered him on and celebrated him as a genius. About his death the following is known: Fortschig had been in a state of more or less constant inebriation since the New Year. Financed by some good-natured private source, he had published a new issue of *Apfelschuss,* a particularly sad specimen, containing an attack against an unknown, probably invented doctor with allegations that have been rejected as absurd by the medical community. He seems to have done this with the sole and wantonly destructive intention of creating a scandal. The fantastical nature of the attack is made evident by the mere fact that the author, while challenging the unnamed doctor with a great deal of pathos in his article to turn himself in to the Zürich police, simultaneously told all and sundry that he wanted to go to Paris for ten days.

"He never got to Paris. He had already postponed his departure by a day, and on Tuesday evening gave a dinner in his shabby apartment in the Kesslergasse to celebrate his imminent departure. His guests were the musician Botzinger and the students Friedling and Sturler. Around four o'clock in the morning, Fortschig—who was very drunk—went to the bathroom, which is situated in the hallway opposite his room. Since he left the door to his study open in order to clear out some of the acrid tobacco smoke that had gathered, the bathroom door was visible to his three guests, who continued to drink at the table without noticing anything unusual. They became alarmed when he did not return after half an hour, and when he did not respond to their calling and knocking, they rattled the lock of the door, but were unable to open it. Botzinger hurried downstairs and asked the policemen Gerber and the night-watchman Brenneisen for help. These two men finally broke open the door and found the unfortunate author dead in a twisted position on the floor.

"Just how this unfortunate event came to pass is still not clear. However, foul play is out of the question, as the city's Examining Magistrate, Dr. Lutz, informed the press at this morning's conference. Although the autopsy appears to suggest a blow with some hard object from above, the physical location of Fortschig's death makes this impossible. The bathroom window, situated on the fifth floor, opens onto a light shaft that is too narrow for a person to climb up and down. Subsequent tests by the police have proved this beyond a doubt. Furthermore, the door must been locked from the

inside, for none of the well-known tricks by which this can be simulated were employed, according to the police experts. The door has
no keyhole and is locked with a heavy bolt. There remains no explanation other than to presume an unfortunate fall on the part
of the writer, which is made all the more plausible by the fact that,
as Professor Detling pointed out, he was drunk to the point of
stupor . . ."

As soon as the old man had read this, he dropped the newspaper.
His hands clutched the blanket.

"The dwarf, the dwarf!" he shouted in the room, for all at once
he had realized how Fortschig had died.

"Yes, the dwarf," replied a voice with a calm, superior air from
the door, which had imperceptibly opened.

"You will admit, Inspector, that I have found myself an executioner the like of which is not easily found."

In the door stood Emmenberger.

THE CLOCK

The doctor closed the door.

He was not wearing the white lab coat he had worn when the inspector had first seen him. Instead he wove a dark striped suit with a white tie on a silver-gray shirt—a carefully groomed appearance, almost dandyish, all the more so since he wore yellow leather gloves, as if he was afraid of soiling himself.

"So now we Bernese are among ourselves," said Emmenberger, bowing slightly before the helpless, skeletal old man. The gesture seemed more polite than ironic. Then he took a chair that had stood concealed behind the curtain, and sat down next to the bed with the back of the chair turned toward the inspector, so that he could press it against his chest and put his crossed arms on top of it. The old man had regained his composure. Carefully he reached for the newspaper, folded it, and put it on the night table. Then he crossed his arms behind his head.

"You had poor Fortschig killed," he said.

"It seems to me that a man who pens a death sentence with such bombastic flourish deserves a lesson in manners," the doctor replied in an equally matter-of-fact voice. "Even writing is getting to be a dangerous profession again. Ultimately it's a good thing for literature."

"What do you want from me?" asked the inspector.

Emmenberger laughed. "That's my question to ask, don't you think? What do you want from me?"

"You know very well what I want."

"Certainly," said the doctor. "I know it very well. And so do you know perfectly well what I want from you."

Emmenberger stood up and went to the wall, looking at it for a moment, with his back turned toward the inspector. Somewhere he must have pushed a button or a lever; for the wall with the dancing men and women opened noiselessly, like a folding door, revealing a spacious room with glass cupboards containing surgical instruments, glittering knives and scissors in metal containers, bunches of cotton, syringes in milky liquids, bottles, and a thin red leather mask—all spotless and neatly arranged. In the middle of the now enlarged room stood an operating table. But at the same time, slowly and menacingly, a heavy metal screen descended in front of the window. The room lit up. For the first time, the old man noticed the neon tubes that were fitted into the ceiling in the spaces between the mirrors. Suspended in the blue light above the cupboards was a large, round, greenish, radiant disk—a clock.

"You intend to operate on me without anesthesia," the old man whispered.

Emmenberger did not reply.

"Since I am a weak old man, I'm afraid I will scream," the inspector continued. "I don't think you will find me a brave victim."

Again, Emmenberger did not reply. Instead he said: "Do you see that clock?"

"I see it," Barlach said.

"It's ten thirty," the doctor said, checking his watch. "I will operate on you at seven."

"In eight and a half hours."

"In eight and a half hours," the doctor confirmed. "But now, sir, I think we have something to discuss. There's no getting around it; then I won't disturb you any more. I've been told people like to be alone during their last hours. Fine. But you're giving me an inordinate amount of work to do."

He sat down on the chair again, its back pressed against his chest.

"I think you're used to that," the old man retorted.

Emmenberger was taken aback for a moment. "I'm pleased," he finally said, shaking his head, "that you haven't lost your sense of humor. Let's start with Fortschig. He was sentenced to death and executed. My dwarf did a good job. Climbing down the light shaft of the house in the Kesslergasse, after a strenuous promenade across wet roof tiles, cats purring all around him, then squeezing through that little window and landing a truly powerful and deadly blow with my car key against the skull of our poetaster on his throne—this was not easy for my little Tom Thumb. I was really on edge, waiting in my car next to the Jewish cemetery, wondering whether the little monkey could pull it off. But the devil is barely three and a half feet tall, and he works without a sound and, most important, invisibly. After only two hours he came hopping back in the shadow of the trees. As for you, Inspector, I'll have to take care of you myself. That won't be difficult, we can spare ourselves further words, which could only be painful for you. But what, for God's sake, shall we do about our mutual acquaintance, our dear old friend, Doctor Samuel Hungertobel?"

"What makes you think of him?" the old man asked warily.

"Why, he brought you here."

"I have nothing to do with him," the inspector said quickly.

"He's been calling twice a day, asking how his old friend Kramer is doing, and wanting to speak to you," Emmenberger said with furrowed brow, looking faintly distressed.

Barlach involuntarily glanced at the clock above the glass cupboards.

"Quite right, it's ten forty-five," said the doctor, regarding the old man in a thoughtful, but not hostile, manner. "Let's get back to Hungertobel."

"He took care of me, tried to help me with my sickness, but he has nothing to do with you and me," the inspector stubbornly replied.

"Did you read the report underneath your picture in the *Bund*?"

Barlach was silent for a moment. He was trying to imagine what Emmenberger's question was aiming at.

"I don't read newspapers."

"It's about your retirement, and it refers to you as a famous local personality," Emmenberger said. "Nevertheless Hungertobel
checked you in here under the name of Blaise Kramer."

The inspector's face was immobile.

"I checked into *his* hospital under that name," he said. "Even if
he had seen me before, he could hardly have recognized me in the
state I'm in."

The doctor laughed. "Are you telling me that you got sick in order to look me up here on the Sonnenstein?"

Barlach did not answer.

Emmenberger looked at the old man sadly. "My dear Inspector,"
he continued, with slight reproach in his voice, "you're not making
our interrogation any easier."

"I'm the one to interrogate you, not the other way around," the
inspector retorted.

"You're breathing heavily," Emmenberger noted with concern.

Barlach no longer replied. All he could hear was the ticking of
the clock. It was the first time he heard it. Now I'll hear it over and
over, he thought.

"Don't you think it's time you admitted your defeat?" asked the
doctor in a friendly manner.

"I don't seem to have a choice," Barlach replied, dead-tired,
pulling his hands out from behind his head and putting them on the
blanket. "The clock. If it wasn't for the clock."

"The clock, if it wasn't for the clock," the doctor repeated.
"Why do we keep going around in circles? At seven I will kill you.
That will simplify the case for you insofar as you can examine the
Emmenberger-Barlach case with me in an objective, unbiased manner. We are both scientists with opposing aims, chess players sitting
in front of one board. You have made your move, now it's my turn.
But there's one peculiar thing about our game: One of us will lose
or else we both will. You have already lost your game. Now I'm
curious to find out whether I will have to lose mine as well."

"You will lose your game," Barlach said quietly.

Emmenberger laughed. "That is possible. I would be a poor chess
player if I didn't count on this possibility. But let's have a closer look.

The odds are all against you. At seven I will come with my knives, and if by some accident that does not happen, you will die of your sickness within a year. But what about my odds? Pretty bad, I admit: You're already on my trail!"

The doctor laughed again.

"You seem to enjoy that," the old man noted with surprise. The doctor seemed more and more strange to him.

"Yes, I admit it amuses me to see myself wriggling in your net like a fly, especially since you're in my net at the same time. But let's look further: Who put you on my trail?"

"I found it myself," said the old man.

Emmenberger shook his head. "Let's move on to more credible things," he said. "As for my crimes—to use this popular expression—you don't just 'find' them; this kind of thing doesn't just fall in your lap. Especially not if you're the Detective Inspector of the Bern City Police. As if I had stolen a bicycle or performed an abortion. Let's look at my case. Since you're beyond hope, you shall be permitted to learn the truth—that's the prerogative of the doomed. I was careful, thorough, and pedantic—in this respect I did a clean, professional job—but despite all my precautions there is, of course, some circumstantial evidence against me. A crime without evidence is impossible in this world of chance. So let's list the possibilities: Where could Inspector Barlach begin? First, there's the photograph in *Life*. I have no idea who took the fantastic risk of shooting that picture; it's bad enough that it exists. But let's not exaggerate. Millions have seen this famous photograph, among them surely many who know me: and yet until now, no one has recognized me, the picture doesn't show enough of my face. So who could recognize me? Either someone who saw me in Stutthof and knows me here—which is rather improbable, since the characters I brought with me from Stutthof are all under my thumb; but, like every coincidence, not impossible, therefore not to be discounted entirely—or someone who, similarly, remembers me from my life in Switzerland before nineteen thirty-two. There was an incident at that time, an experience I had as a young student in an alpine hut—oh I remember it well—it happened under a red evening sky: Hungertobel was one of the five men who were present at the time. It can therefore be assumed that Hungertobel was the one who recognized me."

"Nonsense," the old man firmly retorted. "That is an unjustified idea, an empty speculation, that's all." He sensed that his friend would be in grave danger if he did not succeed in diverting all suspicion from Hungertobel, though he could not quite imagine what this danger would consist of.

"Let's not pass the death sentence on the poor old doctor too hastily. Let's see if there's any other evidence against me; that might exonerate him," Emmenberger continued, his chin resting on his arms, which were still folded on the back of chair. "The business with Nehle. You found that out, too, Inspector, congratulations, it's quite amazing, Dr. Marlok told me all about it. So let's admit it: I myself gave Nehle the scar in his right eyebrow and the burn in his left lower arm, to make us identical, to make one out of two. I sent him to Chile under my name, and when he came home, as we had agreed—this simple-hearted nature-boy, who was never able to learn Latin or Greek but had this astonishing gift for medicine—I visited him in that rickety, crumbling hotel room in Hamburg and forced him to swallow a capsule of cyanide. *C'est ça*, as my beautiful mistress would say. Nehle was a man of honor. He submitted to his fate—I had to push a little, but there's no need to go into that—and he simulated the most beautiful suicide imaginable. Let's forget this scene among whores and sailors, in the foggy dawn of a half-incinerated, half-rotted city, with some lost ships blasting their foghorns somewhere out at sea, a melancholy sound, to be sure. That story was a risky game that could still trip me up rather badly; because who knows what that talented dilettante did in Santiago, and what sort of friends he kept, and who might suddenly turn up here in Zürich to visit Nehle? But let's stick to facts.

"What would be the evidence against me if someone discovered this trail? First of all, we have Nehle's ambitious idea of publishing articles in *Lancet* and the *Swiss Medical Weekly*. That could be a fatal piece of evidence if anyone thought of making a stylistic comparison with my own, earlier articles. Nehle's style was too irrepressibly Berlinish. But to notice that, someone would have to read the articles, which again suggests a doctor. As you can see, things aren't looking good for your friend. Granted, he's unsuspecting. That's in his favor. But when a criminologist joins him—as I'm forced to assume—I'm afraid I can no longer vouch for the old man."

"I am here on a police assignment," the inspector calmly replied. "The German police have become suspicious of you and have entrusted the investigation of your case to the Bern police. You will not operate on me today, because my death would convict you. And you will leave Hungertobel in peace as well."

"Two minutes after eleven," the doctor said.

"I can see," Barlach replied.

"The police, the police," Emmenberger continued, thoughtfully looking at the old man. "It is of course conceivable that even the police might find out about my life, but this strikes me as improbable, because it would be the most advantageous set-up for you. The German police giving the Bern police an assignment to find a criminal in Zürich! No, that doesn't seem logical. I might believe it if you weren't sick, if you weren't in a life and death struggle yourself: for your operation and your sickness are genuine, I can tell as a doctor. And so is your widely reported dismissal from the police force. What sort of person are you? Mainly a tough and stubborn old man who hates to admit defeat and probably doesn't like stepping down either. The possibility exists that you have taken up battle against me privately, on your own, without any support, without police backing, just you and your sickbed, so to speak, because of a vague suspicion that may have arisen in a conversation with Hungertobel, and no real proof. Maybe you were even too proud to involve anyone else besides Hungertobel, and even he seems to be highly uncertain. Your only concern was to prove that even as a sick man you can do a better job than the people who have dismissed you. I consider all this more probable than the possibility that the police would plunge an extremely sick man into such a delicate undertaking, especially since the police up to this hour have not sniffed out the right trail in the Fortschig case, which should have happened if they suspected me. You are alone and are proceeding against me alone, Inspector. I suspect that even that derelict writer didn't have a clue."

"Why did you kill him?" screamed the old man.

"As a precaution," the doctor replied indifferently. "Ten after eleven. Time flies, sir, time flies. Caution requires that I kill Hungertobel, too."

"You want to kill him?" cried the inspector, and tried to sit up.

"Lie down!" Emmenberger commanded so firmly that the sick man obeyed. "Today is Thursday," he said. "That's when we doctors take an afternoon off, as you know. So I thought I would give you and Hungertobel and me the pleasure of a little get-together. He will come here by car from Bern."

"What's going to happen?"

"My little Tom Thumb will be sitting in the back of his car," Emmenberger replied.

"The dwarf!" exclaimed the inspector.

"The dwarf." said the doctor with a confirming nod. "Again and again the dwarf. A useful tool I brought back with me from Stutthof. The silly thing kept tripping me up when I was operating, and according to Herr Heinrich Himmler's *Reichsgesetz* I was obligated to kill the little shrimp as 'unworthy to live,' as if there ever was an Arian giant who was more deserving of life! And why should I have, anyway? I have always loved curios, and a degraded human being makes a most reliable instrument. The little monkey sensed that he owed me his life, and that made him trainable, to my great advantage."

The hands of the clock pointed at eleven fourteen.

The inspector was so tired that he closed his eyes for long moments; and each time he opened them again, he saw the clock, again and again the large, round clock, which appeared to be floating in mid-air. He understood now that there was no way out for him. Emmenberger had seen through him. He was lost, and Hungertobel, too, was lost.

"You are a nihilist," he said softly, almost whispering, into the silent room, in which the only audible thing was the ticking of the clock. On and on.

"Are you saying that I believe in nothing?" asked Emmenberger, and his voice betrayed not the least bitterness.

"I can't imagine that my words could have any other meaning," the old man replied in his bed, his hands helpless on the blanket.

"What do *you* believe in, Inspector?" asked the doctor without changing his position, and looked at the old man with intense curiosity.

Barlach was silent.

In the background, the clock was ticking steadily, the clock, always the same, with merciless hands imperceptibly and yet visibly pushing toward their goal.

"You are silent," Emmenberger said, and now his voice had lost its elegant, playful manner and sounded clear and bright: "Silence. A man of our time does not like to answer this question: What do you believe in? It has become improper to ask that. People don't like to make grand pronouncements, as they modestly say, and least of all to give definite answers, such as: 'I believe in God the father, the son, and the holy ghost,' as the Christians used to answer, proud that they were able to answer. Nowadays people like to keep silent when they are asked, like a girl when she's asked an embarrassing question. Basically one doesn't really know what it is one believes in. It's not nothing, God knows, it's definitely something, though one's notions of it are rather vague, like some sort of inner fog— something like humanity, Christianity, tolerance, justice, socialism, loving one's neighbor, things that sound rather hollow, and people admit that, too, but then they think: It doesn't matter what you call it; what's important is that you live a decent life according to your best conscience. And they'll try to do that, partly by making an effort and partly by letting things drift. Everything they do, their deeds and their misdeeds, happens by chance, good and evil fall into their laps like lottery tickets; it's by chance that one of them turns out well and the other ill. No matter: That fancy word, 'nihilist,' is always at hand as a weapon to throw—with a lot of bluster and even greater conviction—at anyone who makes them uneasy. I know these people, they are convinced it's their right to claim that one plus one is three, four, or ninety-nine, and that it would be unfair to ask them to answer that one plus one is two. Anything that's clear looks rigid to them, because in order to have clarity, you need character. They don't realize that a determined Communist—to use a far-fetched example; for most Communists are Communists the way most Christians are Christians, out of a misunderstanding—they don't realize that a person who believes with his whole soul in the necessity of revolution, and believes that only this path, even if it is paved with millions of corpses, will one day lead to a better world, is less of a nihilist than they are, than some Mr. Müller or Schmidt who believes neither in God nor in the absence of God, neither in hell nor in heaven, but only in his right to make money—a belief that they are too cowardly to postulate as a credo. And so they muddle along like worms in some sort of general pulp that doesn't allow for any decisions, with a nebulous notion of something that is good and right and true, as if there could be such a thing when everything has been reduced to pulp."

"I had no idea that a hangman is capable of such verbosity," Barlach said. "I thought your kind would be sparing of words."

"Good boy," Emmenberger replied, laughing. "You seem to have regained your courage. Good boy! I need courageous people for my experiments in my laboratory. It's a pity my object lessons always end with the death of the pupil. All right, let's see what sort of faith I have, we'll put mine and yours on a pair of scales and see which one of us has the greater faith, the nihilist—since you call me that—or the Christian. You have come to me in the name of humanity or some such idea, in order to destroy me. I don't see how you can deny me the right to this curiosity."

"I understand," replied the inspector, wrestling with the fear that was building up in him, more and more powerfully, more and more menacingly, as the hands of the clock advanced: "Now you want to grind out your credo. It's strange that mass murderers have one too."

"It's eleven thirty-five," Emmenberger retorted.

"How nice of you to remind me," groaned the old man, quivering with rage and impotence.

"Man! What is man?" laughed the doctor. "I am not ashamed to have a credo, I don't shroud it in silence, as you do. Just as the Christians believe in three things that are only one thing, I believe in two things that are really one and the same. I believe that something is, and that I am. I believe in matter, which is *simultaneously* energy and mass, an incomprehensible one-and-allness, and a ball one can walk around, which we can touch and feel like a child's ball, on which we live and travel through the uncanny emptiness of space; I believe in matter (what a shabby, empty thing it is, by comparison, to say: 'I believe in a God'), palpable matter, graspable as an animal, as a plant, or as coal, and impossible to grasp, almost incalculable, as an atom; matter, which needs no God or whatever else you want to invent in addition; whose only, incomprehensible mystery is its being. And I believe that I am—a particle of matter, atom, energy, mass, molecule, as you are—and that my existence gives me the right to do what I want. As a particle, I am just a flash of an instant, a coincidence, just as life in this enormous world is just one of the measureless possibilities, and as much an accident as I am—move the earth a little closer to the sun and there would be no life—and my meaning consists of being *nothing but* an instant in time. Oh the tremendous night when I understood that! Nothing is holy but matter: man, animal, plant, moon, milky way, wherever I look I see accidental arrangements, all of them as insubstantial as foam, or waves on the water; it's neither here nor there whether things are or are not; they are interchangeable. If they are not, something else is. When life on this planet dies out, it will reappear on another planet somewhere in the universe: just as the jackpot always turns up at some point, accidentally, according to the law of large numbers. It is ridiculous to lengthen the span of human life, because it will always be an illusion of duration; ridiculous to invent systems of power in order to vegetate for some years as the head of some state or some church. It's meaningless to strive for the welfare of man in a world that is structured like a lottery—as if it there would be meaning in having each ticket win a penny instead of most of them winning nothing, as if there existed any other yearning but this one: to be, *for once,* that singular, solitary creature, that monster of injustice, who won the lottery. It is meaningless to believe in matter and *at the same time* in some sort of humanism, it is not possible to believe in anything other than matter and the I. There is no justice. How could matter be just? There is only freedom, which can not be earned (for that, there would have to be justice), but that has to be taken. Freedom is the courage of crime, because freedom itself is a crime."

"I understand," cried the inspector, convulsed in his white sheets like a dying animal at the edge of an endless, indifferent road. "You believe in nothing but the right to torture!"

"Bravo!" replied the doctor, clapping his hands. "Bravo! That's what I call a good pupil: one who dares to deduce the law by which I live. Bravo, bravo." (Again and again he clapped his hands.) "I dared to be myself and nothing besides. I devoted myself to that which made me free—murder and torture; for when I kill another human being—and I will do it again at seven—when I place myself outside of every human order that has been erected by our weakness, I become free, I become nothing but a moment, but what a moment! An intensity as huge, as powerful, and as unjustified as matter, and in the screams and in the torment that burst out at me from open mouths and glassy eyes, in the quivering, helpless, white flesh under my knife, I see the reflection of *my* triumph, *my* freedom, and nothing else."

The doctor fell silent. Slowly he rose and sat down on the operating table.

The clock above him showed three minutes to twelve, two minutes to twelve, twelve.

"Seven hours," Barlach whispered almost inaudibly.

"Now show me your faith," said Emmenberger. His voice was calm and matter-of-fact again, no longer hard and passionate.

Barlach did not respond.

"You are silent," the doctor said sadly. "You're always silent."

The sick man did not respond.

"You're silent, silent, silent," the doctor said, leaning both hands on the operating table. "I stake everything on one ticket, unconditionally, I was powerful because I was never afraid, because I did not care whether I was discovered or not. I'm willing to stake everything again, a pure gamble. I will concede my defeat if you, Inspector, prove to me that you have a faith that is as great and as pure and unconditional as mine is."

The old man was silent.

"Say something," Emmenberger continued after a pause, during which he tensely and greedily watched the old man. "Give me an answer. You are a Christian. You have been baptized. Say to me: I believe with a certainty, with a strength that surpasses an abominable mass murderer's belief in matter as the sun's light surpasses a feeble winter moon. Or just this: with a strength equal to that of Christ, who is the son of God."

The clock ticked in the background.

"Maybe this belief is too difficult," Emmenberger said, since Barlach was still silent. He stepped up to the bed. "Maybe you have an easier, more ordinary faith. Say this: I believe in justice and in the humanity this justice should serve. For its sake, and *only* for its sake, have I, who am old and sick, taken upon me this adventure of entering the Sonnenstein, without secondary motives of fame and personal triumph. Say it, it is an easy, decent faith that can still be expected of today's humanity, say it and you are free. I'll be satisfied with your faith, and I'll think, if you say it, that you have as great a faith as mine."

The old man was silent.

"Perhaps you don't believe that I will set you free?" Emmenberger asked.

No answer.

"Say it any way you can," the doctor suggested. "Confess your faith, even if you don't trust my words. Perhaps you can only be saved if you have faith. Perhaps this is your *last chance*, the chance to save not just yourself, but Hungertobel. There's still time to call him. You have found me and I have found you. At some point, my game will be over, at some point my account will not balance. Why shouldn't I lose? I can kill you, I can let you go, which would mean death. I have reached a point from which I can deal with myself as with a stranger. I destroy myself, I preserve myself."

He stopped and looked at the inspector intently. "It doesn't matter what I do," he said, "a more powerful position cannot be attained: to conquer this Point of Archimedes is the highest achievement of which man is capable, it is his only sense in the nonsense of this world, in the mystery of this dead matter, this measureless carrion that keeps bringing forth new life and new death without end. But I bind your release—that is my malice—to a lousy joke, a childishly easy condition: that you show me a faith as great as mine. Show it! Surely faith in the good must be at least as strong in man as faith in evil! Show it! Nothing will amuse me more than to watch my own ride to hell."

The only sound was the ticking of the clock.

"Then say it for its own sake," Emmenberger continued after waiting a while, "for the sake of God's son and your faith in him, for the sake of justice."

The clock, nothing but the clock.

"Your faith," screamed the doctor, "show me your faith."

The old man lay there, with his hands clutching the blanket.

"Your faith, your faith!"

Emmenberger's voice was like brass, like trumpet blasts bursting through an infinite vault of gray sky.

The old man was silent.

Then Emmenberger's face, which had been greedy for an answer, became cold and relaxed. Only the scar above his right eye remained reddened. It was as if he were shaken by some kind of disgust as he turned away from the sick man, tired and indifferent, and went out the door, which closed softly, leaving the inspector enveloped by the glowing blue light of the room, in which only the round disk of the clock continued to tick as if it were the old man's heart.

A NURSERY RHYME

And so Barlach lay there and waited for death. Time passed, the hands of the clock advanced in the circle, came to rest in the same spot, separated again. Twelve thirty passed, one o'clock, five after one, twenty to two, two o'clock, ten after two, two thirty. The room lay there, immobile, a dead space in the shadowless blue light, the glass cupboards full of strange instruments that vaguely reflected Barlach's hands and face. Everything was there, the white operating table, Dürer's picture with the mighty, rigid horse, the metal plate across the window, the empty chair with its back turned toward the old man, everything lifeless except for the mechanical tick-tock of the clock. Now it was three o'clock, and then four. No noise, no moans, no talking, no screams, no steps penetrated to the old man lying there on a metal bed, motionless except for the rising and falling of his abdomen as he breathed. There was no longer an outside world, no revolving earth, no sun, and no city. There was nothing but a greenish round disk with indicators that moved, changed their positions relative to each other, caught up with each other, came to rest in the same spot, strove apart. Four thirty came around, five twenty-five, thirteen minutes to five, five o'clock, one minute after five, two after five, three after five, four after five, six after five. With a great effort Barlach had raised himself to a sitting position. He rang once, twice, several times. He waited. Maybe he could talk to Nurse Kläri. Maybe an accident would save him. Five thirty. He turned his body. Then he fell. He remained lying by the side of the bed for a long time, on a red rug, and above him, somewhere above the glass cupboards, the clock was ticking, its hands pushing on, thirteen to six, twelve to six, eleven to six. Then, dragging himself along with his lower arms, he slowly crawled to the door, reached it, tried to raise himself up, to grab the handle, fell back, lay there for a while, tired again, a third time, a fifth time. In vain. He scratched at the door when he was no longer able to strike it with his fist. Like a rat, he thought. Then he lay without moving again and finally dragged himself back into the room, raised his head, and looked at the clock. "Another fifty minutes," he said into the silence, so loudly and clearly that it frightened him. "Fifty minutes," He wanted to return to the bed; but he felt that he no longer had the strength. So he lay there in front of the operating table, waiting. Around him the room, the cupboards, the knives, the bed, the chair, the clock, again and again the clock, a burned-out sun in the blue glow of a rotting universe, a ticking idol, a face without mouth, eyes, or nose, with two constantly shifting wrinkles that were drawing closer together and were now becoming one—twenty-five to seven, twenty-two to seven—seemed inseparable for a while but were now separating after all . . . twenty-one to seven, nineteen to seven. Time passed, marched on, with faint vibrations in the unswerving pulse of the clock, which alone was unmoving, the magnetic center of inexorable motion. Ten to seven. Barlach half raised himself and leaned his upper body against the operating table, an old, sick man, alone and helpless. He grew calm. Behind him was the clock and before him the door. He stared at it, resigned and humble, this rectangle through which *he* would come, *he* for whom he was waiting, *he* who would kill him, as slowly and as precisely as a clock, cut by cut with his gleaming knives. And so he sat. Now time was within him, the ticking was within him, now he no longer needed to look at the clock, now he knew he had only four minutes to wait, three more, two more: now he was counting the seconds that had become one with the beating of his heart, a hundred more, sixty-more, thirty. So he counted, babbling with white, bloodless lips, a living clock, staring at the door, which opened now, at seven o'clock, with a blow: presenting itself to him as a black cave, a wide-open maw, in the middle of which he vaguely sensed a huge, dark, ghostly presence, but it wasn't Emmenberger; for out of that yawning gorge came a hoarse, scornful rendition of an old children's song:

"*Hänschen klein*
ging allein
in den grossen Wald hinein,"*

sang the piping voice, and in the doorframe, filling it, broad and powerful in a black caftan hanging in rags from his mighty limbs, stood Gulliver, the Jew.

"Greetings, Commissar," said the giant, closing the door. "So I find you again, sad knight without fear or blemish, who set out to fight evil with the power of the spirit, sitting in front of a gurney similar to the one I once lay on in that lovely village of Stutthof near Danzig." And he lifted the old man so that he rested against the Jew's breast like a child, and laid him on the bed.

"Spent!" He laughed when the inspector still could find no words, but lay there, deathly pale. Then he pulled a bottle and two glasses out of the folds of his caftan.

"I don't have any vodka left," said the Jew as he filled the glasses and sat down on the bed next to the old man. "But in a tumbledown farmhouse somewhere in the Emmental, in a crashing storm full of darkness and snow, I stole a few dusty bottles of this stout potato schnapps. It's almost as good. That's permissible for a dead man, isn't it, Commissar? When a corpse like myself—a firewater corpse, so to speak—fetches his tribute from the living by night and fog, as provender, till he crawls back into his tomb in Soviet-land, it's all right. There, Commissar, drink."

Little Hans
went alone
into the great big forest

He held the glass to his lips, and Barlach drank. It felt good, even though he thought it was medically quite unsound.

"Gulliver," he whispered, groping for his friend's hand. "How could you know that I was in this damn mouse-trap?"

The giant laughed. "Christian," he replied, and the hard eyes in his scarred, hairless face glittered (he had drunk several glasses by now). "Why else would you call me to the Salem hospital? I knew right away that you must have formed a suspicion, that maybe the inestimable possibility existed of finding this Nehle still among the living. I didn't believe for a moment that only a psychological interest made you ask about Nehle, as you claimed on that night full of vodka. Was I supposed to let you rush off to disaster alone? We can't fight evil alone any more, like knights setting forth against some dragon. Those times are over. It takes more than a little ingenuity to catch the criminals we're dealing with. You fool of a detective; time itself led you ad absurdum! I never let you out of my eyes, and last night I appeared to our good Doctor Hungertobel in person. I had quite a job on my hands getting him out of his fainting spell, that's how scared he was. But then I knew what I wanted to know, and now I am here to restore the old order of things. For you the mice of Bern, for me the rats of Stutthof. That's how the world is divided."

"How did you get here?" Barlach asked quietly.

The giant's face twisted into a grin. "Not hidden under a seat of the Swiss Railroad Company, as you are imagining," he replied, "but in Hungertobel's car."

"He's alive?" asked the old man, who had finally regained his composure, breathlessly staring at the Jew.

"In a few minutes he will take you back to the old, familiar Salem," said the Jew, drinking the potato schnapps in mighty draughts. "He's waiting in front of the Sonnenstein in his car."

"The dwarf!" screamed Barlach, pale as death in the sudden realization that the Jew could not have any knowledge of this danger. "The dwarf! He will kill him!"

"Yes, the dwarf," laughed the giant, drinking his schnapps, uncanny in his wild raggedness. Putting the fingers of his right hand in his mouth, he produced a shrill, piercing whistle, as if summoning a dog. Then the metal plate covering the window was pushed up, and a little black shadow leaped into the room with a daring somersault, uttering incomprehensible gurgling sounds, glided with lightning speed toward Gulliver, and jumped on his lap, pressing his ugly, ancient dwarf's face against the Jew's tattered chest and wrapping his crippled little arms around the mighty, hairless head.

"Why, there you are, my little monkey, my little beast, my little monster from hell," cried the Jew with a singing voice, fondling the dwarf. "My poor Minotaur, my tortured little gnome, you who so often fell asleep in my arms, weeping and whining, the only companion of my soul in those blood-red nights of Stutthof. My little son, you, my mandrake root. Bark, my crippled Argos, Odysseus returns to you on his endless peregrination. Oh, I thought it was you who sent poor drunk Fortschig into another life, that you slipped down that light shaft, my big newt. Didn't that evil magician Nehle, or Emmenberger, or Minos, whatever his name was, train you for stunts like that in our city of slaves? There, bite into my finger, my puppy! And as I sit in the car next to Hungertobel, I hear a joyful whining behind me, like that of a mangy cat. It was my poor little friend, Commissar, whom my fist pulled out from behind that seat. What shall we do with this poor little beast, who is human, after all, this little man who was degraded to an animal, this little murderer who is the only innocent among all of us, and in whose sad, brown eyes we see the misery of all living creatures?"

The old man had sat up in his bed and looked at the ghostlike pair, the tortured Jew and the dwarf, whom the giant let dance on his knees like a child.

"And Emmenberger?" he asked, "what about Emmenberger?"

The giant's face became like a gray primeval stone, into which the scars had been hammered with a chisel. With a swing of his powerful arm, he hurled the empty bottle into the cupboards, splintering their glass. The dwarf squealed with fear like a rat, leaped across the room, and hid under the operating table.

"Why do you ask, Commissar?" hissed the Jew, but immediately he controlled himself—only the terrifying slits of his eyes sparkled dangerously. With a leisurely gesture, he pulled a second bottle from his caftan and started drinking again in wild draughts. "It makes you thirsty, living in a hell. Love your enemies as yourself, someone said on the stony hill of Golgotha, and let himself be nailed to the cross, and hung on its miserable, half-rotted wood, with a flapping cloth around his loins. Pray for Emmenberger's poor soul, Christian, only audacious prayers are pleasing to Jehovah. Pray! He is no longer, the one you are asking about. My trade is bloody, Commissar, I must not think of theological studies when I carry out my work. I was fair and just according to the law of Moses, just according to my God, Christian. I killed him the way Nehle was killed in some eternally damp hotel room in Hamburg, and the police will conclude that it was suicide just as infallibly as they did then. What shall I tell you? My hand led his hand. Clamped in my embrace, he pressed the deadly capsule between his teeth. Ahasuerus's mouth is sparing of words, and his bloodless lips remain closed. What happened between us, between the Jew and his tormentor, and how the roles had to be reversed according to the law of justice, how I became the tormentor and he the victim—let no one know this except for us two and God, who allowed all this to happen. We must take leave of each other, Commissar."

The giant stood up.

"What will happen now?" Barlach whispered.

"Nothing will happen," replied the Jew, grabbing the old man by the shoulders and pulling him up so that their faces were close together, eye to eye. "Nothing, nothing at all," the giant whispered again. "No one knows, except for you and Hungertobel, that I was here; inaudibly, I glided, a shadow, through the corridors, to Emmenberger, to you, no one knows that I exist, only the poor devils I have saved, a handful of Jews, a handful of Christians. Let the world bury Emmenberger and let the newspapers publish their eulogies and memorials for this dead man. The Nazis wanted Stutthof; the millionaires, this hospital; others will want other things. We can't save the world as individuals, that would be a task as hopeless as that of poor Sysyphus; it is not up to us, nor is it up to any man of power, or any nation, or the devil himself, who is surely more pow-

erful than anyone; it is in the hand of God, who makes his decisions
alone. We can only help in particular cases, we cannot affect the
whole. Those are the limits of the poor Jew Gulliver, those are the
limits of all human beings. Therefore, we should not try to save
the world, but we must endure it. This is the only true adventure left
to us at this late hour." And carefully, like a father with his child,
the giant lowered the old man back into his bed.

"Come, my little monkey," he called, and whistled. With one
tremendous leap, whining and babbling, the dwarf dashed out from
beneath his hiding-place and settled on the Jew's left shoulder.

"That's right, my little murderer," the giant praised him. "We two
will stay together. After all, we're both outcasts, you by nature and
I because I belong to the dead. Farewell, Commissar, we're off on a
nocturnal journey through the great Russian plane, off to venture
a new dark descent into the catacombs of this world, into the lost
caves of those who are persecuted by the mighty."

Once again the Jew waved to the old man. Then he reached with
both hands into the bars, bent them apart, and swung himself out
the window.

"Farewell, Commissar," he laughed again with his strangely
singing voice, and only his shoulders and his powerful naked skull
were visible, and by his left cheek that ancient face of the dwarf,
while the nearly full moon appeared on the other side of the huge
head, so that it looked as if the Jew was carrying the whole world
on his shoulders, the earth and humanity. "Farewell, my knight
without fear or blemish, my Barlach," he said, "Gulliver is moving
on to the giants and the dwarves, to other countries, other worlds,
constantly, without cease. Farewell, Commissar, farewell," and with
that last farewell, he was gone.

The old man closed his eyes. The peace that descended on him
felt soothing; especially since he now knew that Hungertobel was
standing in the slowly opening door, and that he was here to take
him back to Bern.